Dcm 2-2020

OF SPIES

THE SOKOLOV SERIES

The Russian Renaissance
The Collaborator
Temple of Spies
Kremlin Storm

IAN KHARITONOV

TEMPLE OF SPIES

Copyright © 2015 by Ian Kharitonov

All rights reserved. No part of this publication may be reproduced in any form or by any means without the prior written permission of the copyright holder.

Cover design by Hristo Kovatliev.

This book is a work of fiction. Names, characters, places, and incidents either are products of the author's imagination or are used fictitiously. Any resemblance to actual persons, living or dead, or actual events is purely coincidental.

ISBN: 1532972261

www.iankharitonov.com

PROLOGUE

WAR OFFICE REPORT ON BOLSHEVIK ATROCITIES IN RUSSIA

Presented to Parliament by Command of His Majesty.
November, 1918.

1. The Bolsheviks have established a rule of force and oppression unequalled in the history of any autocracy.

2. Themselves upholders of the right of free speech, they have suppressed, since coming into power, every newspaper which does not approve their policy.

3. The Bolsheviks have abolished even the most primitive forms of justice. Thousands of men and women have been shot without even the mockery of a trial, and thousands more are left to rot in the prisons under conditions to find a parallel to which one must turn to the darkest annals of Indian or Chinese history.

4. They continue to hold on to power by a system of terrorism and tyranny that has never been heard of. With fiendish cruelty, the Bolsheviks have begun to operate a plan of systematic extermination. They perform wholesale massacres, the most barbarous methods of torture and the odious practice of taking hostages.

5. The number of Corean and Chinese units is reported to be increasing in Bolshevik forces. The sole object of these units is plunder, as they are merely bandits and not a regular army. No one wants to join the Red

Army now except the worst elements of the people. If a conscript deserts, his parents or wife are treated with extreme brutality. The Bolsheviks who destroyed the Russian army, have forcibly mobilised officers who do not share their political views, but whose technical knowledge is indispensable, and by the threat of immediate execution have forced them to fight against their fellow-countrymen in a civil war of unparalleled horror. At Pskoff, 150 Russian officers who were taken prisoners by the Red Guards were given over to Mongolian soldiers, who sawed them in pieces.

6. The Bolsheviks vent violent hatred on church and clergy, pillage monasteries, persecute and murder priests and monks. Churches and graves have been desecrated. A bishop was buried alive.

7. The avowed ambition of Lenin is to create civil warfare throughout Europe. Every speech of Lenin's is a denunciation of constitutional methods, and a glorification of the doctrine of physical force. Bolshevism in Russia offers to our civilisation a menace, and until it is ruthlessly destroyed we may expect trouble, strikes, revolutions everywhere. For Bolshevik propaganda unlimited funds are available. No other country can give their secret service such a free hand, and the result is that their agents are to be found where least expected.

RED TERROR

Siberia, 1920

The Hungarian commissar, Balázs Kurilla, holstered his revolver as he strode away from the church, leaving bloodstained footprints in the snow. The villages behind him burned down, bathing him in a devilish glow, every house set on fire. The clotted blood covering his calf boots matched the crimson pentagram on his leather cap. His Bolshevik superiors had tasked him with instilling a reign of terror, and they would be pleased with the results. He and his Red Guards had indulged themselves in a frenzied feast of rape, murder and pillage, sparing no one. He, Balázs Kurilla, would have no mercy for the enemies of the Revolution. Outside the church, a few hundred corpses lay piled seven rows high, their limbs intertwined in macabre stillness. Kurilla had personally shot several families of well-to-do peasants, their bodies now hidden somewhere at the bottom of the gory heap.

A group of Red Guards filed out of the church, looting icons, holy vessels and ornaments which they added to a string of carts stashed with their plunder. Their mismatched sheepskins, now adorned with red ribbons to signify their Bolshevik allegiance, had also been requisitioned from the eliminated Russian vermin.

Through the cocaine-induced haze clouding his brain, Kurilla noticed three Lettish guards up ahead. They stood over the prone figure of an old priest, kicking him. He cowered, reciting a prayer in defiance. Then the Letts began to smash his bones with the butts of their rifles. Instead of breaking into a scream, the priest's voice grew stronger as he praised the Lord. The unwavering faith angered his assailants, who intensified their blows.

"Enough!" ordered Kurilla, approaching. "Step aside!"

The Red soldiers complied. Kurilla yanked the rifle from one of them and waved all three away. Looming over the priest, he saw not a severely injured, bleeding old man, but 'an element of the most reactionary class' which had to be eradicated. Icy wind tugged at the priest's white beard and simple black cassock as he struggled to rise to his feet.

Kurilla reached out and ripped the gold crucifix off the old man's neck. Furiously, he then raised the rifle and bayoneted the priest in the stomach.

The Russian priest let out a muted cry.

"Where is it?" said Kurilla. "The gold."

"You've ... taken it all. There's no more! ... The icons!"

Kurilla retracted the bayonet and thrust it again into the same wound. The priest gasped in shock as he sank to the frozen ground.

"No. Not your worthless icons. The gold. *Five hundred tons of gold.* Where is it?"

Despite the pain, incredulity crossed the priest's wrinkled face.

Through gritted teeth, he rasped, "I know nothing!"

Kurilla stabbed him again and again into the wound, thirteen times.

But through the agony, the priest only murmured his prayer.

Frustrated, Kurilla turned to the Lettish guards.

"Get me those new Russian conscripts."

Barking orders, the Letts brought the two young Siberian peasants who had only recently enlisted in the Red Army. Stability in the Red ranks depended on the well-paid Lettish and Chinese mercenaries, and the proportion of Russian soldiers had to be kept to a minimum to avoid unrest.

Wearing cast off clothes, each looked filthy and emaciated. The two conscripts had joined the Bolsheviks for food, so this would be their first real test.

Kurilla tossed the rifle to one of them.

"Finish that old vermin!"

The young Red soldier leveled the rifle, blood dripping from the bayonet, but was unable to pull the trigger. His hands trembled. Tears streamed down his sunken, pallid cheeks. His knees buckled and he dropped the rifle.

"No! I can't! Please, comrade, no!"

Kurilla grabbed his revolver and shot the Russian in the forehead. In a puff of red spray, he toppled to the ground.

Pointing with the revolver, Kurilla addressed the second man.

"Pick up the rifle and do it!"

Paralyzed by fear, the peasant did not move. Then he took off his worn-out hat and crossed himself religiously.

Kurilla fired, killing him on the spot.

Cheers erupted from the crowd of Red Guards who stood watching, drawn by the spectacle.

Kurilla surveyed the scene, stroking his ginger mustache.

The priest was still alive.

A short man stepped forward. He wore an overcoat with a red star-shaped badge on the sleeve. He had a feline face and savage eyes. The front and top of his head were shaved and the rest of his hair was braided in a pigtail. He was a Chinese mercenary named Wu Xiaodong, the most sadistic butcher Kurilla had ever met. For his ruthlessness, the Bolsheviks paid Wu the highest wages in the Red Army.

With disdain, Kurilla threw the crucifix away and stared at the golden-domed church. The gold would haunt him until another day. He nodded to Wu.

The Chinaman scampered toward the priest who attempted to crawl away, clawing at the snow. Stamping on his wound, Wu stripped the old man naked and bound his hands and feet with a length of rope. On his command, a mob of his fellow Asian mercenaries—Mongols, Koreans and Chinese—swarmed all over the priest. Together, they dragged the old man through the snow back into the church, where they had already set up a huge iron cauldron to boil him alive.

THE NOVITIATE

Moscow, 1943

After an overly made-up secretary ushered Valdemar Vasiliev inside the office and closed the door behind him, he felt trepidation. He had been brought to the Lubyanka with extreme urgency, so he had no idea what to expect. It was the blackest hour of the night. Only a desk lamp illuminated the office. Its glow cast an eerie light on a portrait of Comrade Stalin himself. Coils of cigarette smoke drifted from the dwarfish, curly-headed, bespectacled man sitting behind the desk as he pored over a manila folder. Like Vasiliev, he was clad in the khaki-colored uniform of the NKVD, but he far outranked the young operative.

Vasiliev snapped to attention in front of his superior.

"Comrade Colonel! Lieutenant Vasiliev reporting as ordered!"

Colonel Isaac Edelman eyed the lieutenant, sizing him up.

"Ah, Vasiliev. Please, sit down."

Valdemar Vasiliev strode across the vast room, his heels clicking on the wooden floor, and occupied the chair opposite the walnut desk.

Edelman proffered a silver cigarette case.

"Do you smoke?"

"Negative, Comrade Colonel!"

Edelman smirked. "Don't worry, this is American quality via Lend-Lease. Only the very best from our Western allies."

"No, thank you, Comrade Edelman."

"A healthy lifestyle! Good. You are indeed a fit athlete. I can see that you rightfully deserve the top marks you received from our very own Dynamo sporting society. And I gather you're an excellent marksman as well."

Edelman closed the file and put it aside, placing it on top of a stack of identical folders.

It was *his* file, Vasiliev realized.

"Well then, Lieutenant, I must inform you that you have been picked for a mission that will greatly serve the Soviet Union and the glory of communism. A mission sanctioned by our great leader, Comrade Stalin."

Involuntarily, Vasiliev glanced behind Edelman at the lamp-lit portrait of their Master.

"You are no doubt aware," Edelman continued, "that as the world's most progressive proletarian society, we have successfully battled the opiate of religion poisoning the minds of workers and peasants. Namely, the most harmful and delusional cult of them all—Christianity."

Vasiliev nodded. He knew that the fiercest enemy of communism, the Orthodox Church, had been practically wiped out. Since the start of the Revolution, out of the 150,000 Russian clerics, approximately 120,000 had been exterminated. But for a handful, the rest would soon die rotting in prison.

"However..." Edelman crushed his cigarette in an ashtray crammed with butts. "This religious hydra has spawned again despite our best efforts. Churches have been reopening across the Soviet territory occupied by the Germans. But our valiant Red Army will soon smash the fascist invaders. And we will flush out every German spy and lackey everywhere, including the churches. Meanwhile, we are conducting an operation under the direct command of Comrade Andrei."

'Andrei' was the alias of Pavel Sudoplatov, the head of the NKVD Sabotage Division. One of Stalin's closest servants, Sudoplatov had earned legendary status in NKVD ranks after orchestrating the assassination of Trotsky in Mexico.

"It is called Operation Monastery. And you, Lieutenant, are just the kind of operative we need to accomplish the mission. You and many others like you working behind enemy lines. You will pose as an aspiring priest or monk—a novice—and infiltrate one the Russian churches. Is that clear?"

Lieutenant Vasiliev straightened in his chair. His chest swelled with pride.

"Comrade Colonel, I will do everything to justify your trust!"

"I am sure of it. You're a fine Bolshevik, as was your father."

"Yes, Comrade Edelman, he fought the reactionary clergymen in Siberia."

"Of course, he was one of the Latvian Red Guards. I shouldn't forget that Vasiliev isn't your real name, but your father's alias.

How ironic. You will now get to pick your new name as you become a novice. Choose wisely. Something that you can become comfortable with. You will have to use it for a very long time."

"A few months?" Instantly, Vasiliev regretted his error. For certain, the Red Army would sweep the Germans away shortly, no matter what the sacrifice. Doubting the Red Army's success sounded criminal. But above all, he should not have inquired about the duration of a top-secret operation. His excitement was no excuse for letting that slip off his tongue.

Stone-faced, Isaac Edelman produced another American cigarette from his silver case and lit it, exhaling smoke contentedly. Then he smiled.

"No, not a few months. You should be prepared for a far longer period in the undercover role of a priest. I would say ... the rest of your life."

Astounded, Vasiliev kept himself from asking any more questions that could cost him.

"We will reclaim the Russian land," said Edelman. "And we will reclaim the Russian churches. But this time, we will keep them for ourselves."

PART I

1

Thailand

The bodysnatchers arrived to collect the corpse like they always did, ahead of the police. Hundreds of them prowled the moonlit streets of Bangkok, waiting for accidents to happen. They operated all around the city, always ready to react as they listened to radio chatter. This time it was a dead body found floating in a canal, one of the city's numerous *khlong* waterways. Within minutes of receiving the report, the nearest Toyota pickup truck patrolling the area had raced to the *khlong*. Getting out of the Toyota, a team of two hurried to the scene, their yellow coveralls bearing the stenciled logo of the Phyo Ba Kyu Foundation.

A forty-six-year-old accountant by day, Jaidee worked as a night-time volunteer helping out during emergencies. His partner, Porntip, was a twenty-year-old waitress. Lacking a public ambulance service, Bangkok depended on the large-scale work of private organizations such as the PBK Foundation. The volunteers, also known as bodysnatchers, rushed the injured to hospitals or picked up the dead.

In his three years at the Foundation, Jaidee had seen his share of accidents, mostly car crashes with drunk motorists, locals and tourists alike, returning from bars and nightclubs. Although he earned no money from his nocturnal part-time job, he received something far more valuable in return. The entire staff of volunteers acted on the Buddhist principle of karma, hoping that their efforts in the present life would be repaid after reincarnation. Similarly, the entire PBK Foundation existed only on donations from people who thus wanted to boost their karmic virtue.

As he and Porntip approached the canal, Jaidee saw that some positive karma had already taken effect. To his delight, none of PBK's competitors had shown up. Turf wars still broke out between rival charity groups, especially now that anti-government protests had swept areas of Bangkok, making teams of bodysnatchers avoid them for fear of being attacked.

Stepping on a creaky wooden platform at the water's edge, Jaidee trained his flashlight on the body. The drowning victim bobbed face-down in the murky, putrid water of the canal. Washed up with bits of trash polluting the *khlong*, the body had stuck between the wooden struts of the platform.

A police siren sounded in the distance. The arrival of a cruiser drew a few curious onlookers to the canal as Porntip spread out a bed sheet on the platform.

Pulling the corpse out of the water proved to be a struggle. Jaidee had to use every ounce of his strength to tug the unusually bulky body onto the cloth, aided by Porntip and the policeman.

Catching his breath, Jaidee examined the body. Dressed only in track pants, the Caucasian man lay like a grotesque wet mannequin, his skin waxen. With the muscular build of an athlete, he must have weighed around a hundred kilograms, and was just under two meters tall.

"No sign of foul play," said Jaidee. "Just another accident."

"Pack him for the morgue." The policeman nodded and left. There was nothing else for him to see. Drownings in the canals occurred all too frequently.

Latex-gloved, Jaidee patted the dead man's pockets. The corpse carried no valuables. No wallet, no watch, no jewelry. Porntip scowled, visibly upset. Thai families at least made generous donations for finding the bodies of their relatives. With this foreigner, the case seemed unlikely.

Jaidee shared both her disappointment and her dislike for tourists. The only item that he recovered from the body was a Russian passport issued in the name of Eugene Sokolov.

2

The CIA man swore profusely as the Iranian fired the first shot.

From his position, Tom Frey observed the SWAT team move in with lightning speed against the backdrop of multi-colored containers and towering cranes. For the Texas-born intelligence officer, several months of intense work was now concluding in Laem Chabang Port.

Located between Bangkok and Pattaya, Laem Chabang ranked as one of the busiest commercial ports in the world. The container traffic passing through Thailand's main sea hub measured in the millions, but Frey only wanted twelve specific units stacked amid the endless rows of the B1 terminal. On the verge of busting a weapons-smuggling deal between Iran and North Korea, he was leading the joint operation personally. It was a chance he couldn't miss. The North Koreans had chosen Laem Chabang as a transit point in an elaborate deception involving multiple vessels en route from Nampho to Bandar Abbas. Frey had known the date and place of shipment for weeks, but an anonymous tip-off had indicated that the respective envoys from both sides would be present to hand over the containers. He was going to catch them red-handed as they met to conclude the transfer.

Frey frowned as he tightened the grip on his Beretta, watching the action unfold. Deep lines etched his forehead. His receding hair and growing gut conspired to make him look a decade older than his real age. He was entering the twilight of a career which had begun years ago in Seoul, and he was desperate to end it on a high. He would *not* let it slip.

The casually dressed suspects, three Iranians and two North Koreans, panicked as they found themselves surrounded by Arintharat-26, the Special Operations Unit of the Royal Thai Police. The Iranian higher-up barked a command in Farsi to his two subordinates as he whipped out a handgun and opened fire at the advancing Thai team. A North Korean also drew his semi-automatic as his comrade took flight.

None of them stood any chance against the special unit. The armor-clad members of Arintharat-26 scythed them down with a storm of bullets from Heckler & Koch MP5 submachine guns. The Iranians dropped dead, their skulls cracking open like ripe melons from the well-placed head shots. A salvo killed the gun-wielding North Korean even before he could pull the trigger. His running comrade stopped in his tracks and crashed down as slugs tore into his back.

The firefight had ended in a flash. The Arintharat-26 men secured the area in the vicinity of the containers and their team leader gave the all-clear signal.

"Dammit," Frey muttered as he came over to inspect the carnage.

All five arms-traffickers lay in pools of blood. The grisly sight coupled with the thick, smoggy air made Frey feel like he was suffocating. The armored vest on top of his long-sleeved shirt and tie didn't help, either.

"You okay?" asked a Thai-accented voice behind him. "You don't look too happy. Lots of blood, eh?"

Chatchai, the liaison from Thailand's Department of Special Investigation, joined Frey on the scene. At six feet tall, Frey towered over the short Asian. The Thai cut a portly figure and his soft, chubby features made him a man of indeterminate age. Perspiration on Chatchai's shaved scalp glistened in the sun. With his fleshy cheeks and protruding ears, Chatchai reminded Frey of a laughing Budai figurine sold in souvenir shops.

"Yeah," Frey admitted. "I wanted to catch at least one of them. Alive."

Chatchai shrugged. "We won."

For a small fish in a small pond like Chatchai, seizing the arms shipment was more than enough. It constituted a domestic triumph that would propel his DSI career further. The global war on terror appeared to be peripheral to his personal glory.

Frey nodded, but in his mind he rued the outcome of the operation. His gut feeling told him that the shipment was merely a piece of the puzzle. Now all possible links to the grand scheme had ended up sprawled on concrete, pumped full of lead and very much dead. Standing over the body of the lead Iranian, Frey identified him as Hossein Azizi of the Islamic Revolutionary

Guards. Just where and when Azizi's terrorist group had intended to use the weapons, and for what purpose, Frey would never learn. Yet witnessing Azizi's death had provided a measure of consolation.

Chatchai gave the order to open up the first twenty-foot-long container, splattered with Azizi's blood. The Arintharat men cut the metal locks and inspected the cargo labeled as drilling equipment. Inside one of the crates, they uncovered a batch of grenade launchers, fresh off the production line of a North Korean arms factory.

Chatchai beamed like a Cheshire cat. "Tom, just look at this!"

Cheering, he shook Frey's hand.

Just then, a harried Arintharat officer addressed Chatchai.

"Sir, one of the perpetrators is alive!"

Frey spun around and rushed toward another Thai operator who was keeping an eye on a prostrate North Korean several meters away from the containers.

The runner.

Covered in blood, peppered with slugs, he was still breathing, groaning in agony.

"Hot damn."

Frey couldn't believe his luck. Snatching the North Korean spy could blow the lid off the arms deal and expose the entire terrorist network.

He turned to Chatchai.

"Listen carefully," he told the DSI man. "You and your men will make no mention of this bastard's existence in your reports. You've only seen four bad guys. Three Iranians, one North Korean. Not this one. No big deal. Nothing else changes. Understood?"

Chatchai's black eyes darted from the wounded Korean back to Frey.

"I have no idea who you are talking about. I never saw him."

"Good. Now get me your car over here before he kicks the bucket."

"Do you think he's transportable?"

"He'd better damned well be. The hell I will let him die without telling me everything he knows first."

Then, in a last-gasp act of desperation, the North Korean summoned whatever stamina he had left. He sprang to his feet and launched himself at the Arintharat officer. A strike with the stock of the MP5 knocked the wind out of the resilient smuggler in an instant, and the officer zip-cuffed him.

"On the double, Chatchai!" Frey commanded. "Looks like the bastard got some beans to spill. He'd rather get shot than start talking. But I'll make him talk, whatever it takes. He's mine now."

3

The post-9/11 war on terror had given rise to CIA secret prisons around the world, known as black sites. The unrestrained use of black sites had allowed the CIA to employ abduction and torture as intelligence-gathering techniques against terror suspects. Under the covert interrogation program, detainees would be whisked away to any of the black sites scattered across Afghanistan, Iraq, Morocco, or most notably, Eastern Europe: Poland, Romania, Lithuania. But the earliest black site, which would spawn the CIA's global network of clandestine facilities, had been located in Thailand. Code-named 'Cat's Eye,' a warehouse in the north-eastern Thai province of Udon Thani had housed the CIA's first high-value prisoner and Al-Qaeda leader, Abu Zabaydah. Other black sites had also existed elsewhere in Thailand, including one at the Don Muang Royal Thai Air Force base outside Bangkok.

While the majority of black sites had been shut down, a nondescript building on the outskirts of Pattaya remained fully functional. Hidden in plain view on an ordinary street, the single-story structure did not appear any different from the houses surrounding it. No security forces protected it, no sign denoted it as property of the Thai government. Only a simple fence isolated the tiny plot of land it stood on, overgrown with tropical shrubs and short palm trees.

Inside, the North Korean spy lay on a cot, unconscious, his wounds cleaned and bandaged. The ceiling fan stirred the odor of antiseptics around the Spartan room, mixing it with the air's hot dampness. A strand of Frey's dark hair stuck to his sweaty forehead.

"So, how long has he got?"

Kerry Gwinn, an American doctor on the CIA payroll, drew a curt, exasperated sigh.

"Your guy has a bullet lodged in tissue from the penetrating gunshot wound to the thorax, but I don't think the lung was hit. He should be diagnosed properly, however. I believe there's internal bleeding and intestinal damage from the second bullet. It entered his posterior left flank near the twelfth rib and exited through the abdomen. This could mean very bad news. If he doesn't bleed to death, he'll die of severe infection. He needs immediate hospitalization and surgery."

"That's out of the question, Doc. He knows enough for his own comrades or Azizi's men to come after him. Either they'll kill him as soon as he shows up near a hospital, or they'll vanish from Thailand by the time I get the chance to interview him. He's staying put."

"In that case, his prognosis is bleak. I'm warning you that if he doesn't undergo laparotomy in the next eight to twelve hours—"

"Ample time for me to squeeze the intel out of him."

"In his current condition, you shouldn't expect much. His blood pressure is dropping. As he suffers circulatory shock, he won't be able to respond to your questions."

"I'll take the gamble. Nothing to lose. Just get him into some sort of shape. Like you said, there's not much time to waste."

Frey's tone ended all further debate.

Giving up, Gwinn injected the Korean with a stimulant.

Frey paced the stuffy room, clenching his fists nervously. His plan was going to hell. He still hoped to extract some useful information from the prisoner before his physical state deteriorated further. Such extreme methods as waterboarding did not seem worthwhile, as he was unlikely to survive it. Frey would have to rely on chemically assisted interrogation. It hardly guaranteed success, but even a long shot was worth a try. Barring a miracle, the captive spy would take his secrets to the grave. His non-official cover made it almost impossible to identify him and trace his contacts.

Three minutes later, the Korean blinked rapidly. He groaned, attempting to move, but the pain paralyzed him. With a deft hand, Gwinn administered an intravenous shot. It was a short-acting narcoanalysis drug which produced a psychoactive effect in less than a minute.

"The hypnotic trance will wear off quickly," Gwinn cautioned.

Frey pulled up a chair and sat next to the cot.

He shouted, "*Neo! Ireumi mwoya?*" *You! What's your name?*

The Korean's lips moved, his voice barely audible.

"Lee."

Frey continued in fluent Korean. "I know that you're a spy from the North. At Laem Chabang, you were involved in the illegal transfer of weapons to Iranian terrorists. Right now, you can obtain medical attention and a new life courtesy of the American government. All you have to do is provide the details of your arms-smuggling deal—"

Lee emitted a moan which grew into a guttural cry.

"Father! ... Father!"

He stared blankly at the ceiling, beads of sweat running down his face.

"Listen to me, Lee! Give me the name of your handler!"

Instead of answering, Lee kept repeating the word over and over again like a mantra.

"He's delirious," Gwinn said. "It's no use."

Then, Lee yelled out in English.

"Father! The priest!"

Frey bolted from his chair.

"The hell are you talking about? What priest?"

"The priest! ... I need to see him! ... Dionysius. Father Dionysius. The All Saints Church in Pattaya. The Russian priest!"

Lee mumbled groggily as his voice faded. Then he passed out.

Frey grabbed him by the shoulders and shook him.

"Take it easy!" Gwinn intervened, holding Frey back. "You won't get anything else from him."

Livid with rage, Frey kicked the chair.

"Worthless bastard!"

He had reached a dead end and he knew it.

Getting hold of himself, he realized that he possessed a single lead to work on.

The priest.

If Lee somehow knew him, then the priest could also know something about Lee.

Still, Frey didn't get his hopes up. It was far more likely that the Korean had been babbling complete nonsense. The drug's influence often yielded fantasies instead of valuable data. Frey was clutching at straws, but it was his last resort. He had to dial Chatchai again.

4

As it turned out, the Russian priest was not Russian at all. Father Dionysius had Oriental features and a complexion to match. Even his facial hair, mandatory for Orthodox Christian clergy, grew in tiny whiskers. The full-length black cassock, long-sleeved and loose-fitting, looked incongruous with the frail Asian man wearing it in such excessively hot weather. Seemingly still in his twenties, he appeared remarkably young for a holy father.

As he got out of Chatchai's Nissan, Tom Frey showed the confessor inside the house. Frey felt no risk in bringing any visitor to the black site, let alone a priest. By design, the house gave away nothing out of the ordinary. Frey showed him into the room where Lee lay dying.

"Do you know that man?" Frey asked.

Father Dionysius shook his head.

"How did he know about *you*? He asked to see you specifically."

"A lot of people come to our church to find peace," the priest answered in English.

With him, Father Dionysius carried a small bag which contained his communion kit. Frey scrutinized the priest as he went through his ritual. Himself raised a Roman Catholic, Frey couldn't remember when he'd last gone to church, but he stood mesmerized by the ancient ceremony. Although he wasn't too religious, Frey acknowledged that Christian tradition had transcended millennia and offered a sense of continuity. He was witnessing a liturgy that people had performed centuries before his birth and would continue to do so centuries after his own death.

On the chair next to the cot, Dionysius laid out his utensils. Frey recognized some of the objects which were similar to those in the Western Mass. Atop a veil, the priest placed the ciborium, a receptacle for carrying the Sacrament bread and wine, and lit a candle. Then Father Dionysius recited a prayer in Slavonic as he poured wine into a golden chalice, mixing it with the Eucharistic bread.

"I must ask you to leave," he told Frey. "Absolution can only be granted in private. It is secret. You may return later."

Frey slipped into an adjacent room, where Chatchai sat behind a laptop. The display showed a video feed from the other room. The hidden surveillance equipment would record every word between Dionysius and Lee. Frey would get his confession one way or the other.

The priest opened a prayer book and read from it in a booming voice. He continued reading for several minutes.

"Just get on with it," Frey said, growing impatient.

Lee lay unmoving, his breathing shallow.

Dionysius approached Lee with the chalice.

"What sins do you wish to confess?"

Lee uttered a single word.

"Cowardice ... "

He would speak no more. A short silence fell.

"Do you accept to take the Sacrament?"

"Yes," Lee rasped.

Praying loudly, Dionysius held the chalice and brought a spoonful of the Sacrament to the North Korean's lips.

Another prayer followed. Subsequently, Father Dionysius collected his items, placing them back into his travel pouch as he prepared to leave. Frey cursed, chagrined at his failure. The entire procedure had proved pointless. Back to square one.

At Frey's prompt, Chatchai re-entered the room and offered to drive the priest back to the church.

"No, thank you. I can find my way. The Lord will guide me."

No sooner had he said it than the priest exited the house and simply vanished.

Twenty minutes later, the North Korean prisoner died.

5

Lee Young-Hwan of the DPRK Cabinet General Intelligence Bureau died with a sense of defeat. He deserved nothing else but death. Yet he welcomed his punishment. He had failed the Party by allowing himself to be captured alive. Death served as a consolation that did little to negate his failure.

The poison acted quickly. Mixed with the bread and wine, the cyanide had enough dosage to kill him in minutes.

His death became unimportant. He had prepared for it. He would have died of his wounds anyway. Only the way he died mattered now. Taking the poison would end his suffering and grant his family a chance for survival. By contacting his handler, he had shown his loyalty. He had proven that he had not betrayed the Party. He had not defected. He had told the enemy nothing.

Dionysius would send a message back to North Korea for the government to spare Lee's wife and two children.

Or so Lee hoped as he took his last breath.

Dionysius ...

6

After Dr. Gwinn had confirmed Lee's death, Frey ordered Chatchai to dispose of the body. An autopsy and the resulting backlash of a formal investigation were inconceivable, not that Frey deemed it necessary to determine the cause of death for a guy shot by a special operations unit. As soon as Chatchai's clean-up team arrived, Frey left the black site. This time the nondescript house outside Pattaya would shut down for good.

Everything was over. Frey had done his job in Thailand. He had busted the arms deal, and the rest should have been of no concern to him. Acting beyond his immediate objective hadn't paid off.

Frey felt too exhausted to drive back to the U.S. Embassy in Bangkok. Nightfall neared. The notorious Bangkok traffic, aggravated by the Red Scarf protests, made the hundred-mile journey impractical. Instead, he asked Gwinn to drop him off in downtown Pattaya. He ignored the massage parlors en route. The red-light district would have made his blood rush at a younger age, but now the brothels and bars of Walking Street did not appeal to him.

He checked in at a three-star seaside hotel. He ate a hearty meal of coconut-milk tom yam and chili tiger prawn curry, spicy enough to make his eyes water, and washed it all down with a pint of Tiger draft beer. Later, he went to his room, finding it reasonably tidy. A cool breeze wafted in from the spacious balcony. Frey salvaged a couple of Jack Daniels minibar bottles and nestled himself into a chair. The liquor, the star-filled sky and the serene night view of the beach outside all soothed him.

Frey's phone buzzed. He answered.

"It is done," said Chatchai.

"Good." Frey toasted with the mini bottle.

"Are you in Bangkok?"

"No, in fact I'm still in Pattaya."

Chatchai snickered. "Having fun with the ladyboys?"

"Oh shut up. Something's bothering me about that priest. Dionysius."

"Really? What exactly?"

"I think he lied. They knew each other. The priest is hiding something."

"Have you had too much alcohol, Tom?"

"Damn you, Chatchai. I just want to have a word with him."

"I don't see any point. He barely speaks any English."

"I bet he'll be more talkative with a fellow Thai. Do me a favor."

"He's not Thai."

"Who the hell is he, then?"

"I have no idea. What does it matter? Lee's dead. Case closed. Enjoy your triumph. I got a busy day tomorrow. Good night, Tom."

Frey sat in his chair and drained another whiskey in a single gulp.

It didn't add up. A Russian priest in Thailand who was neither Russian nor Thai. *What if he isn't even a priest?*

Besides, North Korea remained the world's number one persecutor of Christians. While it was possible that Lee had kept his faith secret to avoid a firing squad, he was first and foremost a North Korean officer. Worshiping Christ seemed irreconcilable with serving the very government that exterminated Christian believers. *If he wasn't a Christian, then why did he demand to see Dionysius?*

Dionysius. That wasn't his real name. Orthodox clergy adopted new names as they entered priesthood, much like each Catholic Pope took a regnal name.

Like Chatchai said, the routine case should have been done and dusted, but it got more confusing instead, given the circumstances of Lee's death. Without doubt, Lee and his North Korean comrade at Laem Chabang had been low-level spies. The real facilitator of the arms deal was still out there somewhere, the eminence grise pulling the strings.

Eminence? Priest?

Frey's thoughts jumbled together.

He stepped out on the balcony and peered at the coastal lights of the city's vibrant nightlife. Pattaya remained the first-choice destination for sex tourism. And located somewhere between the thousands of go-go bars and nightclubs, amid the debauchery of transgender prostitutes and preying pedophiles, stood the All Saints Church of the Russian Orthodox denomination. How bizarre, Frey thought. Who on earth would want to build a church in a place dubbed Sin City?

Surreal.

Something clicked in his mind. A sense of foreboding overcame him.

He picked up his phone again and sent an encrypted message to Langley. He requested all available data on the activities of the Russian Orthodox Church in Thailand. A hell of a long shot, but over the years, checking every fact had become second nature to him.

Rummaging the minibar, he retrieved a vodka and an orange juice. He mixed the two.

Hardly had he finished his screwdriver when the reply from Langley came in.

As he started reading the report, it made his skin crawl. Surreal was an understatement. What he saw was plain crazy.

"Hot damn."

7

Chatchai lit a cigarette to calm his nerves but his pudgy fingers trembled. He always felt edgy in the presence of Bangkok's night overlord, Song Dae-Ju.

The upper-level private lounge of a go-go bar in Silom had a smoking balcony which overlooked the dance floor. Psychedelic music blared from the jam-packed area below, luminous from strobe lights flashing shades of blue, pink and purple. Scantily clad working girls swarmed among the patrons, offering themselves alongside the overpriced drinks. Dancing rhythmically, on-stage performers entertained the partying crowd.

Chatchai felt none of the excitement emanating from the dance stage. Dread gripped him under Song's fierce glare. What made it especially chilling was the heterochromia. The right eye was brown; the left had a light hazel hue, almost gold.

Song possessed a demonic air about him. His hair layered in bangs and dyed red, a short black jacket on his bare torso, ripped muscles bulging. And those piercing eyes, sucking the soul out of Chatchai.

"No survivors. That was the deal. You screwed up at Laem Chabang."

Chatchai swallowed.

"But—but... it's all right now," he stammered. "Lee is dead. No survivors."

"Your ineptitude forced Dionysius to risk exposure. Now the American is nosing around."

"There's no way he can prove that Father Dionysius poisoned Lee. I got rid of the body myself."

"Proof isn't necessary. Attention can be damaging enough. A chink in the armor, allowing a lethal blow. We have already suffered a serious setback with the detection of that arms shipment."

"I'm sure it's only a minor upset. Nothing of the sort will happen again. The way you handled the whistle-blower will strike fear into the hearts of others. The American should not pose a threat. He's clueless."

The multi-colored eyes narrowed in contempt.

"For your own sake, I hope you're right. Even if Frey figures out what he's dealing with, it'll be too late. I've already contacted Moscow. Dionysius will be gone tomorrow..."—a flick of the wrist to consult his rose-gold Omega—"*today*, rather. It won't matter then. Meanwhile, enjoy the night. And always remember to serve me well, or you'll end up floating in a *khlong*."

As he departed, Song Dae-Ju tossed a small plastic token in Chatchai's direction. Chatchai caught it.

A blue-colored casino chip. His pay. It had no value denoted, no markings except a large letter *B* on each side.

Chatchai knew however that it was worth ten times his salary at the DSI.

8

He needed no dojo, no gym, no partner to practice his moves. Solitude enhanced his focus. His rigorous training did not even require any special equipment—nature had provided him with everything. He used large rocks for weights and the trunk of an apple tree in lieu of a punching bag. Concentrating in a deep *shiko-dachi* stance, he struck the leafless tree with bare hands and feet. From perfect stillness, his body exploded to deliver lightning-fast blows. His mind channeled his energy into each strike, feeling no pain upon impact with the stiff, hard wood. His starched, white *gi* rustled, held tightly by his fourth-degree black belt. The black belt was embroidered with his name, hand-stitched in golden katakana script.

Due to the phonetic peculiarities of the Japanese language, it did not perfectly match the Russian-sounding *Sokolov*.

Nothing was perfect, but he strove for perfection with each strike against the tree. Hundreds, thousands of strikes to polish his technique and, above all, forge his spirit.

The garden was his training ground and his home. It was all that remained of his dacha in the countryside near Moscow. The loghouse built by his father had burned to the ground in an attack which Sokolov had survived only by the grace of God. He had neither the money to restore the old house, nor the desire to do it. In a recent thousand-kilometer trip down south, he had discovered the original Sokolov estate, ransacked and neglected for decades. His brother, Constantine—a historian—had learned that the mansion of their forefathers had been destroyed by the Bolsheviks almost a century before. The southern estate of their Cossack ancestors couldn't be brought back. Similarly, Sokolov decided, should he attempt to restore his father's house outside Moscow, it wouldn't be the same. His memory of it sufficed. He had no time to live in the past.

But he still had the garden, which had stayed intact, and the sky above him, the color of his azure eyes. The patch of land around him was spacious enough to perform his *kata* routine freely. A few naked trees surrounded him. An evergreen forest loomed beyond.

He completed his workout, his *gi* soaked through. His breath came in puffs of vapor. Late autumn approached; temperatures were dropping. The ground felt cold under the withered grass as he walked back to his dwelling.

He lived inside a semi-trailer attached to a massive KAMAZ truck. A twin orange-blue stripe ran along its side, painted in the color scheme of EMERCOM, Russia's militarized counterpart of the American FEMA. The semi-trailer was a state-of-the-art mobile command post. Employed by EMERCOM for disaster response, the mobile command post was equipped with satellite phone and Internet comms, two-way radio, EMERCOM intranet, and an auxiliary electrical generator in addition to a connected power line. The eight-by-two-meter body was coated with super-efficient ceramic insulation. Sokolov climbed in, embraced by the warmth of electric heating.

Growing up at a Soviet airbase in East Germany, he'd seen far worse conditions.

The semi-trailer was divided into four compartments: office, bedroom, kitchenette and bathroom. Lavishly furnished with a leather chair and sofa, walnut desk and cabinets, a high-end wall-mounted TV, the mobile command unit signified its occupant's high rank within the government agency. Indeed, Eugene Sokolov commanded EMERCOM's Extra-Risk Team, the elite rescue unit deployed for the most dangerous missions.

After Sokolov's house had burned down, General Klimov, the EMERCOM boss, had donated the mobile command post to his best officer for temporary use.

Nothing is more permanent than the temporary, Sokolov thought.

As he traversed the oblong section, the desk phone rang.

The EMERCOM hotline.

He picked up the corded handset.

"Gene," said Klimov, his voice tense. "Get ready. The matter is urgent. Sergei will pick you up in ten minutes. The plane is on the runway."

Abruptly, Klimov hung up.

Sokolov proceeded without deliberation. His job required absolute subordination. Human lives depended on his actions. For now, Klimov had told him everything he needed to know. He would have the details later.

He showered and changed into his EMERCOM uniform, sapphire-blue with an orange beret. Lacing his boots, he looked at the dial of his Breitling Superocean chronometer. Nine minutes had elapsed.

He exited the semi-trailer and heard the distant sound of a rumbling diesel. A Land Rover Defender approached, also painted white with the twin orange-blue EMERCOM stripe. Sokolov's right-hand man, Sergei Zubov, sat behind the wheel. No sooner had Sokolov got in the passenger seat than the Defender made a sharp turn and drove back toward the highway.

Neither tall nor athletic, head shaved, brow furrowed, his face craggy and long-nosed, Zubov looked the complete opposite of his commander. But he and Sokolov weren't just team-mates, they were closest friends who trusted each other with their lives. Zubov drummed his fingers on the steering wheel nervously. Sokolov knew him well enough to sense that something was bothering him deeply.

"What's going on, Serge? I'm off duty this week."

"It's an off-duty assignment."

"Unofficial?"

"Our agency has been asked for a favor by that other agency. In no uncertain terms."

Sokolov sighed. "Bastards."

"Klimov is under a lot of pressure from the SVR." Zubov referred to the Russian foreign intelligence service.

"What do they want?"

"They want us to save their skins."

"We're rescuers all right, but they must have misunderstood the notion."

Zubov shrugged. "They want us to clean up their mess, whether we like it or not."

"So what's this mess we're getting ourselves into?"

"I only know the gist of it. Their guy blew his cover or something. They want us to fly in and get him out."

"Destination?"

"Thailand."

"I see. He can't do it on his own because of the riots. All of the Thai airports have been closed."

"Exactly. And we're going in under the official pretense of a relief mission. Like, helping out the poor Russians stranded in Thailand. Tourists, diplomats, their families, take your pick. In reality, we're only bringing back the SVR guy."

"Why us, though? The Extra-Risk Team? Sounds like a mundane mission for any crew."

"Let me explain. EMERCOM is in good international standing due to our humanitarian program. The aid we provided to Thailand following the 2004 tsunami has not been forgotten. An inbound EMERCOM flight won't raise any eyebrows, unlike a Russian military plane. But also, the Thai authorities must save face. They want to avoid diplomatic backlash after the dead body of a Russian tourist showed up in a Bangkok canal. So the Thai government would rather grant us permission to land than face a scandal."

"And that's our smokescreen."

Zubov nodded. "Klimov thought you'd be the best man to settle the incident. As a matter of fact, the corpse carried a passport issued in your full name. Eugene Ivanovich Sokolov."

"What a weird coincidence."

"Coincidence or not, the passport holder also shared your date of birth."

"Curiouser and curiouser."

"The embassy guy meeting us there will fill you in."

Sokolov found the news disturbing. Whether the man found dead in Bangkok had been an unlikely namesake or an unfathomable impostor, his personal involvement in the affair felt almost fatalistic.

They reached the EMERCOM airbase. A gleaming white Ilyushin transport jet with orange-and-blue markings awaited on the tarmac, engines running.

"The exfiltration should be straightforward," said Sokolov. "We fly in, grab the spy and deliver him to Moscow. Am I right?"

"Well ... Here comes the worst part. It's not Russia that we must take him to. It's North Korea."

9

Restless, Tom Frey waited for the sun to rise. He re-read the memo again, overcoming his initial disbelief.

There were *six* Russian churches in Thailand.

Pattaya held not one but *two* of them.

The idea of Russian tourists going on a pilgrimage to Pattaya stretched credibility. Neither Thais nor Westerners, who made up the majority of visitors to the country, had any use whatsoever for one, let alone two or six.

The Russian expat community in Thailand measured in far too insignificant numbers to warrant such a strong clerical presence. What purpose did the churches serve?

The answer stung Frey as he studied the list of parishes. Using their secular names, he had requested additional data for each priest and combined the results. What he had least anticipated was getting hits as he ran their real identities through all available military records.

To his amazement, each and every one of them was on file.

1. St. Nicholas Chapel. Bangkok. Priest: Archimandrite Theodore, secular name Vadim Savin. Retired Sergeant, Russian Airborne Troops, 76th Air Assault Division, with over thirty combat missions in Chechnya.

2. Holy Trinity Church. Phuket. Priest: Hierodeacon Flavian, secular name Georgi Kirienko. SVR Colonel, retired.

3. Holy Dormition Monastery. Rachatburi Province. Priest: Hieromonk Agathangel, secular name Vladimir Melnik. Retired Captain, Russian 58th Army, 19th Motorized Rifle Division, involved in the 2008 South Ossetia War.

4. Holy Ascension Church. Koh Samui. Priest: Father Seraphim, secular name Dmitry Shatsky. Former GRU officer, 22nd Guards Spetsnaz Brigade. Infiltrated Crimea with an illegal paramilitary group to support the Russian annexation. Suspected of fighting in the war against Ukraine as part of covert invasion force.

5. Church of the Protection of Mother of God. Pattaya. Priest: Hieromonk Nicander, secular name Boris Babich. Graduated cum laude from the Soviet Institute of Marxism-Leninism, degree in Atheism. Previously appointed to the Orthodox Cathedral in Havana, Cuba.

Could it be? Using the church as a front for clandestine operations?

It was not by any means unheard of. Tales of diabolical papal intrigues dated back to the Middle Ages. But to think that in the twenty-first century, modern-day spies were disguising themselves as clerics ...

No matter how far-fetched, the pattern emerged clearly. Four priests with Russian military or special forces background, and one devout communist welcomed by Castro's oppressive regime as a Christian missionary. The mysterious Cold War connection did not end there. None of the church staff were local Thais. The Russian priests were assisted by immigrants from Laos, Cambodia, Vietnam—all former communist or socialist countries.

Frey never jumped to conclusions without hard evidence, yet he found no other logical explanation for the data. The bigger picture needed cross-checking. For the moment, it could wait. Whatever rotten was going on in the Russian Church, it wasn't his current priority. He got the result he needed. The *sixth* parish on the list.

It was the final entry which had stunned him the most.

6. All Saints Church. Pattaya. Priest: Father Dionysius, secular name Ri Kwang-Hyok.

The name produced only one known match in the database. There could be no mistake.

Special Battalion, Reconnaissance Agency of the Korean People's Army.

Many Koreans often had matching full names. Tom Frey kept that cultural phenomenon fully in mind but he left nothing to coincidence. Beyond doubt, it was the same man. The man known as Dionysius was serving on active duty in North Korea's special operations unit.

10

A landscape of tropical vegetation and paddy fields appeared in view during descent. The EMERCOM cargo plane landed at Don Muang before the sun reached its zenith, yet the heat was perceptible. The warm temperature presented a welcome change from the bleak, overcast chilliness of Moscow. Humidity hung in the air but the monsoon season had passed. The clear sky promised excellent conditions for the return leg with almost no chance of rain.

Two men greeted Sokolov: a Thai general and a Russian diplomat. Introductions were made, pleasantries exchanged.

David Kinkladze wore a short-sleeved shirt and tie, gray trousers and blue Ray-Ban Aviator sunglasses and carried a leather bag. As a Russian spy, Kinkladze worked under the official embassy cover of a cultural attaché.

General Udomkul bared his yellow teeth as he spoke.

"Welcome to Thailand, Major Sokolov. I assure you that your crew will have full cooperation from the ground staff."

"Thank you, General," Kinkladze interjected. "We appreciate your friendship and the growing rapport between our great nations. The plane should be refueled and ready for take-off by the time Mr. Sokolov and I return with our passenger."

"Is our arrangement still in place, Mr. David?"

Kinkladze shot the Thai official a stern glance.

"You need not worry, General. Trust my word."

Sokolov made a mental note of the exchange as he followed Kinkladze to the embassy car. It was a black metallic Toyota Crown Royal with tinted windows and diplomatic license plates. Kinkladze climbed into the driver's seat on the right.

With Sokolov sitting in the back, Kinkladze chauffeured him to Bangkok. It wasn't the first time Sokolov had visited a country with left-hand traffic, but the odd feeling of driving in the wrong lane took a while to shake off.

"First up," the attaché said, "we have to check out that dead guy. A funny story, if you ask me."

"What's so funny about someone dying?"

"Oh, he's got your name. He even looks like you. Same name, age, hair color, height, weight, build, all very similar. The catch is, here in Thailand, last names are unique to each family. Thais don't share a surname unless they are related. So it's amusing. Kind of. That dead guy is definitely not you, but are you sure he's not your brother or something?" Kinkladze chuckled.

"My brother is alive and well, thanks for your concern."

"Yeah, huh, good. That's what I want you to say at the coroner's office. Instead of transporting the body back to Russia, we'll leave it unclaimed and unidentified. I'll do most of the talking, you just nod, okay? Afterwards, we can forget about the whole thing. Then we go and pick up the passenger."

"So, is the passport fake or genuine?"

"That's a tough question."

"What is that supposed to mean?"

"Don't tell anyone, Major, but it's damned easy to get a real Russian passport in a false name. You can get one in Moscow for about three or four thousand bucks, American. The prices are competitive. That money buys you a forged Russian ID, which you then use to apply for a genuine Russian passport. Just make sure you opt for the plain old variety which doesn't have the machine-readable biometrics chip with your fingerprints, eye retina scan or whatever. Nonetheless, it's an honest-to-goodness Russian passport, valid for ten years. Choose any name to your heart's content, even Donald Duck, nobody will bat an eyelid. That's just one way to obtain it. Throw in hundreds of lost passports which are reported each year by tourists. These can be doctored by crooks easily. Even blank passports get stolen from embassies."

Or get sold by crooked diplomats, Sokolov thought.

"Are you saying there's an entire market for this sort of thing?" he asked, feigning ignorance.

"You bet. Especially here in Thailand. Lots of people want to protect their privacy, you know. Anonymity is in high demand these days."

11

Tom Frey drove to the All Saints Church. He'd contacted Langley and reported his findings but the reply was taking too long and he had no time to waste. Similarly, the embassy station chief had no field men at his disposal to assist Frey.

"I advise extreme caution in the current highly volatile political climate," the diplomat had told him.

Damned politicians, the lot of 'em.

Frey was determined to take the matter into his own hands and locate Ri Kwang-Hyok, also known as Father Dionysius. He'd deal with whatever happened next on his own terms. There wasn't a problem that his Beretta and a few spare clips couldn't solve. Even if he was making a mistake—which was *impossible*, he told himself—he had to act on the lead he'd unearthed. He was not going to let that one slip from his grasp. Hell no.

He found the Russian church closed. It was located in a deserted blind alley, concealed amid tropical trees and shrubs away from the nearest street. The secluded position reminded Frey of a black site.

He hid behind the foliage on the other side of the street. He waited in ambush for almost an hour, but nobody showed up. The church—a three-storied building which resembled a colonial-style villa with domed cupolas attached on top—stood locked and seemingly abandoned.

The Kim-Jong-Un-lovin' bastard hightailed it out of Pattaya, Frey thought. *He knew I'd be coming for him.*

Frey took out his phone. He debated on calling Chatchai but decided against it. He'd do it alone. He was hot on the North Korean's heels. He had to keep up the chase. Frey was by no means a trigger-happy gunslinger but the thrill of the hunt made his heart pound. Dionysius thought he had fooled him, but now Frey was coming after him.

Bangkok. Frey had to get there, the sooner the better. The St. Nicholas Chapel. The enemy's lair.

All the answers lay there. And this time *he* would be the confessor.

12

Sokolov had witnessed death numerous times. The morgue in Bangkok hardly differed from any other around the world. But he had never encountered something so unexpected as he was shown the corpse of the drowned Russian.

The dead face was waxen, mannequin-like, yet still recognizable.

He hoped his eyes were playing tricks on him. He had to be wrong.

"Do you know this man?" asked a bespectacled Thai official.

"No," Sokolov lied. His voice did not betray his surprise.

Kinkladze took over the conversation.

"Thank you for informing us about the death of a Russian citizen. As you can see, we have attempted to find the next-of-kin without success. We'll continue our search, but frankly, I don't believe that anyone else will claim the body. Mr. Sokolov here is in no way related to the man in question. However slim the odds, I'm glad we got it out of the way. Mr. Sokolov also happens to represent the Russian government. The main reason he's here is to verify the cause of death and coordinate the financial requirements arising from the body's disposition."

"The forensic examination determined the cause of death as drowning. The full autopsy report will be available within three months. I'll make sure that your embassy receives it. As for the disposition of the remains, I understand that you see no reason for repatriation?"

"Unless we find the next-of-kin," Kinkladze said. "And I assure you that it's highly unlikely at this point. We've already done our best."

"In that case, no additional mortuary expenses will accrue. The remains will be cremated and buried at a private graveyard.

The PBK Foundation—the volunteers who found the body—will do it free of charge."

"Excellent. Our business is done, then. Thanks again for your help. *Khob khun krap.*" Kinkladze bowed and turned to leave.

"*Khob khun krap! Sawasdee krap.*" The Thai bowed back.

"What about the personal effects?" Sokolov asked.

"*Chai krap.* But of course! I must pass them over to you. Please wait."

A minute later, the Thai official returned carrying a small plastic bag. He handed it to Sokolov.

It contained just two items.

The ill-fated Russian passport.

And a blue casino token.

13

He had met Alexei—or 'Alex'—Grib at a mixed martial arts tournament in Poland, seven years before. Alex, a Belorussian *sambo* fighter, had always favored dirty tricks, hitting his opponents in the neck and groin areas. When Sokolov knocked him down twice in the first round, Alex had gone mental, trying to gouge Sokolov's eyes. Sokolov had knocked him out. Disqualified by the referee and subsequently banned from competitive fighting, Alex had instigated a nightclub brawl and faced charges of rape on the next day. He'd fled from prosecution back to Belarus and nobody had heard from him ever since.

Not until he'd stolen Sokolov's identity, perhaps to avoid arrest.

Sokolov didn't bother telling the story to Kinkladze. For starters, Sokolov couldn't be one hundred percent certain it was him, no matter how striking the resemblance of the ghostly face. He'd seen Alex in the flesh only once before. Seven years had passed. Secondly, assuming the dead man was indeed Alex Grib, nobody would mourn his demise. And finally, the death of anyone other than a Russian national wouldn't interest Kinkladze in the slightest. Nothing mattered to Kinkladze apart from reaching the St. Nicholas Chapel to pick up his spy.

Through heavy traffic, Kinkladze navigated the streets of Bangkok, careful to bypass the districts paralyzed by the riots. At one junction, Sokolov glimpsed a police cordon holding off a seething throng of protesters. All of them wore red bandannas and yelled out slogans, incited by their leaders. The unruly crowd threatened to clash with the armed policemen, the two sides separated by coils of barbed wire laid across the road. Red flags waved, drums thumped, bullhorns blared with angry, hysterical shrieks. Cursing, Kinkladze turned from the bottleneck to a small alley.

The St. Nicholas Chapel was unlike anything Sokolov had expected to set his eyes on. He could hardly call it a chapel at all. Instead, it was a single-story shed with an image of the Virgin painted above the door and a couple of crudely-constructed crosses stuck on the roof like TV aerials. A clumsy wooden sign did proclaim it as a Russian Orthodox church, nonetheless. The tiny yard between the front gate and the church entrance was cluttered with assorted flower pots, a water hose, an empty bucket, and a broken motorcycle covered by tarpaulin. Rundown Thai homes neighbored it, surrounded by rust-eaten fencing.

Kinkladze stopped the car in the middle of the littered alley. He waited behind the wheel, reluctant to venture out in the stinking heat. He stole glances at the dashboard clock.

"Where the hell is he?" Kinkladze said. "We arranged to meet here without delay."

Kinkladze left the car and approached the low sliding gate before the shack-like chapel. He pressed the buzzer. No response. He held the button again, insistently.

Finally, a man emerged from the back of the house. An Oriental with matted hair, dressed in a checkered shirt, baggy pants and flip-flops, was lugging a gym bag with great strain. Kinkladze motioned for him to hurry up. The Korean scurried past Kinkladze, who stayed behind to lock the gate with his own key.

Stuck in traffic at an intersection, Tom Frey paid the cab fare and proceeded on foot. The polluted air and the humidity made him sweat from exertion as he walked the distance to the designated street.

He failed to spot the church. The tell-tale onion dome was nowhere to be found. He peered at the English-dubbed street sign, which gave him the correct name.

Abruptly, he detected something else, and realized that he shouldn't have been looking for a Russian church where there wasn't one.

Hurrying from a house which had a slapdash cross jutting atop its roof, was the man he'd come for.

Dionysius. Or rather, Ri Kwang-Hyok. Gone were the dignified black cassock, the golden crucifix, the ceremonial demeanor. The Korean now bore more resemblance to a vagrant than a holy father as he walked over to a waiting Toyota.

Frey gained pace, reaching for his holstered Beretta. The car's tinted windows made it impossible to discern if another passenger occupied the rear seat. Frey fancied his chances, regardless.

"Hey, you!" he shouted. "Hold it right there, you son of a bitch!"

Blocking his path to the car, Frey grabbed Dionysius by the lapel and jabbed the gun into his ribs. With a shocked expression, he dropped his gym bag and gaped at Frey.

Behind the Korean, another man—an Eastern European—rushed forward to intervene. Frey recalled his face from a file listing Russian SVR personnel in Thailand. Frey shoved him back. The Russian staggered and fell.

Dionysius kicked out at Frey, trying to break free desperately, so he smacked him across the face with the butt of the Beretta.

Just then, a looming figure came into view.

A red bandanna masked his face. He held a gun, leveling it at Frey.

Frey swung his Beretta.

Alerted by the commotion in the narrow street, Sokolov turned to see what was going on. To his amazement, a gun-wielding heavyset Caucasian was attacking Kinkladze and the Korean. The situation was getting out of hand. Sokolov had to sort it out before it turned ugly. He reached for the car door.

Suddenly, two gunshots thundered in quick succession.

Through the tinted glass, Sokolov watched the Korean and his assailant topple, spewing blood. Their masked killer switched his aim to Kinkladze. The SVR man cowered. Another shot blasted. Blood erupted from Kinkladze's forehead and he crashed down.

The killer discarded the gun and took flight, moving swiftly as he jumped over a fence and ran between houses to an adjacent street. His red bandanna would help him blend into the crowd of protesters. Sokolov had no chance to distinguish his hidden face. But he would never forget the killer's eyes, different in color. Dark brown and light hazel.

14

One minute. The fine margin between success and failure—life and death—couldn't have been more pronounced. Song marveled at the workings of fate as he waded through a roaring mass of protesters, indiscernible in the crowd.

Sixty seconds later, Kinkladze would have taken Dionysius away, never to be found by the CIA. Frey would have finished his search empty-handed. Song wouldn't have had to kill all three of them.

No matter. The outcome satisfied him. He had solved the problem for good. Dispatching Alex Grib and then Lee had proved insufficient. Now he had eliminated all danger completely: Dionysius, his Russian handler, and the meddlesome American.

For a few days, the tabloids would spin their deaths into a juicy backpage story, playing into Song's hands. A rendezvous between a CIA spy and his Russian counterpart gone awry, killing an innocent bystander, some unknown priest.

No links could be traced, the true meaning of the murder scene impossible to deduce.

Nothing—and *nobody*—could jeopardize his operation.

15

Sokolov held his emotions in check. He had to act professionally. He stepped out of the car and examined the gruesome picture. Three lifeless bodies lay sprawled on the ground. Three clean head shots indicated the work of a trained hitman.

Sokolov scanned the alley. The booming gunfire had attracted a few frightened neighbors.

The Toyota's engine idled. He weighed the alternatives. No point in giving chase, he reasoned. The killer had vanished out of sight. The police would sooner start chasing *him*. Refuge at the Russian embassy didn't present a viable option. Trying to explain Kinkladze's death would complicate matters further. The last thing on his mind was giving himself in to an angry SVR spy section who would likely blame him for the death of their comrade.

Leave the country first, deal with the authorities later. His first priority lay in getting his two team-mates out of Don Muang safely.

As he got in the right-sided driver's seat, he pulled out his rugged Sonim phone and dialed Zubov.

"Sergei? It's me. Tell Mischenko to prepare for take-off. Right now. I'm coming back, alone."

"Is anything wrong, Gene?"

"*Everything* is wrong."

Wary of the traffic flow, he drove out of the alley and dashed around a maze of streets. If only he could find the way back to Don Muang. The diplomatic plates granted him immunity from the police, for the time being. Irate motorists honked as the Toyota cut in front of them, darting between lanes sharply. He had to reach the motorway as fast as he could. He remembered the general route but the chaotic traffic, aggravated by the protests, made him feel trapped.

He had walked into a trap right from the start. In some mystical way, Alex Grib's death had led him into it. But for a moment's hesitation, he would now be lying dead on the ground, detected and shot by the killer. He felt determined to play no part in whatever spy game the SVR was running.

As the traffic slowed to a crawl, Sokolov snatched Kinkladze's handbag. The Toyota lacked a navigation system, and Sokolov's old-school phone had no GPS chip.

Delving into the handbag, he was taken aback by the contents. Two bundles of cash, ten thousand U.S. dollars each, made for an unusual discovery. He put the money aside and dug deeper. He had to unzip a hidden compartment to find what he was looking for.

He fished out a portable device. Lightweight, the mid-sized tablet fitted comfortably in his hand. The gadget had a clean, sleek design, dominated by the screen. The thin bezel around it contained no elements apart from the power button. Oddly, the manufacturer logo was absent. He spotted neither a fingerprint scanner nor a facial-recognition camera, so he tried his luck. Chances were that the device had no security protection.

Struggling to keep his eyes on the road, Sokolov powered on the no-name slate. The operating system booted quickly, requiring no PIN-code entry. He expected to find some mapping software among the stock applications, but his hopes evaporated once he saw the main screen.

The tablet ran on custom firmware, the likes of which he had never encountered. The minimalist user interface featured no icons, widgets or buttons. The display remained blank for a few seconds.

Against a black background, white text popped up.

`Welcome to the Dark Web`

Two multi-colored options appeared below.
    EXIT, in blue.
    ENTER, in red.

16

Sokolov tapped on EXIT.

The tablet powered off.

He booted it up again, and was shown the same start screen.

Welcome to the Dark Web

This time, he pressed ENTER.

A text field appeared, prompting input on a virtual keyboard.

Once more, two choices presented themselves beneath. Blue and red. EXIT and ENTER.

Sokolov had no idea what any of it meant. Was he supposed to enter a password?

The Dark Web? What the hell?

The tablet equally baffled and intrigued him. There must have been a reason Kinkladze had kept it. Could it possibly be a spy gadget? Sokolov wondered. Too unorthodox for an SVR communications device. Strangely sophisticated and mysterious.

Sokolov could think of only one person who might give him the answer.

He dialed Pavel Netto, the EMERCOM tech whiz back in Moscow.

The traffic was easing. Sokolov neared the outskirts of Bangkok.

After several rings, Netto answered in a sleepy voice.

"Yes, boss?"

"Pavel, I have a little problem here. I need your advice."

"Go ahead, I'm listening." Netto stifled a yawn.

Sokolov assumed that Netto had just woken up in his room, surrounded by all sorts of geeky clutter. Netto was the ultimate spiky-haired nerd who probably even slept at his desktop, keyboard in hand. He was the go-to guy for anything that existed in the hi-tech world, or was yet to come into existence.

"Do you know anything about the Dark Web?" Sokolov asked.

A long pause ensued at the other end.

"Pavel? Did you hear me?"

Finally, Netto spoke, sobered.

"*My God.* Eugene, I beg you, whatever you're up to, just stay away from it."

"The Dark Web. What *is* it?"

"I'm not sure you'd want to know. There are things you wish you could forget. It's one of those."

"It's vital that I know it first. Tell me."

Netto sighed.

"Give me a second to figure out where to start."

"You don't have a second. Three men have died before my eyes in a second."

"All right! Jesus, that's terrible. Okay, listen. Visualize the entire Internet. A few hundred million domains. From massive sites like YouTube, Facebook, Twitter, stuff like file-sharing, video downloads, down to blogs, and what not. Tens of billions of pages crawled by Google. Terabytes, Petabytes, Exabytes of data."

"Exabytes? It's hard to grasp. But I do get the fact I can have anything within a click."

"Right. Now try to comprehend that this size of the Internet which you can access every day is just the tip of the iceberg. This insanely colossal wealth of information created by mankind makes up only a minuscule fraction of what is actually stored online. Imagine that there is a *hidden* Internet which is five hundred times bigger."

"Hidden?"

"The Dark Web. Deep Internet."

Sokolov hit the brakes a fraction of a second before the Toyota hit the car bumper ahead of it.

"Unbelievable. Five *hundred* times *bigger?*"

"If your regular Internet is a vast ocean surface, then Deep Internet is the underwater habitat."

"You're not kidding, are you? What's it like down there?"

Netto's reply filled Sokolov with dread.

"Wonderland. It's like stepping through the Looking-Glass. An alternative world. Total freedom, total anonymity."

Kinkladze's words echoed. *Anonymity is in high demand.*

"In other words, a cloak for illegal activities," Sokolov said.

"Yes and no. More often than not, anonymity is a cloak *from* illegal activities. The Dark Web is a place where the NSA won't track your every move. The mega-corporations won't spy on you. Tyrannical governments won't intercept your chat messages and forum conversations. Remember, the Dark Web contains a copy of the conventional, public Internet which you can still browse. Also, it has all the content which is otherwise paywall-protected. Subscription services, music, movies—all available instantly. That's the freedom part. And a lot of the information there is just raw data, hosted on private servers, not arranged in website form. But yeah, due to its incognito nature, there are certain areas ... " Netto hesitated. "Some of the stuff on Dark Web is just ... *sick*."

Sokolov made it to the highway. A final stretch of the road separated him from Don Muang.

"Any examples?" he asked.

"Gene, honestly, you shouldn't stir up a hornet's nest. It's pure evil. I'm nauseous even thinking about it. Child pornography. Pedophile scumbags and all sorts of perverts flock there like it's their promised land, knowing they'll never risk punishment. Not just child porn; bestiality, incest and so much other vomit-inducing depravity, the amount is staggering. But that's not all. You can buy any drugs at marketplaces like Silk Road. Heroin, cocaine, meth, LSD, you just add any quantity to cart and check out like it's goddamned Amazon or something. In fact, you can buy *anything*, no matter how illegal. Prostitution rings function openly—again, offering even underage hookers."

"You're right, Pavel, I'm sick to my stomach."

"Whatever you want to find, and more than you bargain for. It's all there. Some things you later wish you could unsee. But you get the full range of crazy stuff. Hackers like me who discuss computer virus creation with their peers. Underground betting syndicates that fix results in English football. Illegal fighting circuits where contestants battle to the death. Assassins for hire. Terrorist organizations and the intelligence agencies hunting them. Financial empires and cryptocurrency traders."

"Hang on, do you mean this Dark Web of yours has its own *banking* system?"

"Of course. Have you heard of Bitcoin? It originated from the Dark Web as one of its many payment methods for unregistered transactions. The Dark Web is a great venue for untraceable financing."

"Wonderland," Sokolov muttered.

"Like I said. Mind-boggling, terrifying, containing the world's entire knowledge and the answers to all of life's questions. The truth behind every conspiracy. The classified information that sometimes gets leaked to the media has been known in the Dark Web for years. "

"How do I access it?"

"It can be daunting for a complete noob, but you're more or less computer-literate."

"What a compliment."

"First, you need to download a special browser. One that supports incognito web surfing through anonymous connections."

"I already have it."

"Excellent. You're making great strides. Next, you need to type in a particular web address. Your gateway to the Dark Web. A secret key to a secret door."

"Which address is that?"

"I'm getting to it, wait. The public Internet uses such domains as dot-com, dot-org, dot-net, and so on. Deep Internet, on the other hand, is accessed through dot-anon. The Dark Web links won't work unless you have the anonymizer extension, and the web addresses are cryptic, consisting of random characters. I'll text you the link. Your portal to the other side. Hang in there, Gene. Ring me up if you need any more help."

The call ended.

Sokolov struggled to concentrate on the road. His mind reeled as the phone conversation with Netto sank in. What he'd just learned gave sense to the bizarre tablet, its software built entirely around the anonymous browser, Sokolov now realized. The device had no other purpose than surfing the Deep Internet, hence the limited design and functionality. But he'd come no closer to understanding Kinkladze's use for it.

Child porn? Underage prostitutes?

Sokolov cringed.

The phone buzzed with an incoming text message.

8CmSgi2.anon

Typing as he drove precariously, he copied the link into the address field of the Dark Web browser.

His finger hovered over the ENTER button. A single press away from taking the plunge, he felt anxious. Did he really want to know what lurked behind the Looking-Glass?

He glanced at the casino chip retrieved from Alex Grib's body, and noticed the letter *B* marking it. Bitcoin? Whether he liked it or not, he had been sucked neck-deep into that whole mess. Perhaps he needed to go deeper to push himself off the bottom and break out. Find the reason for killing Kinkladze.

He hit the red button. ENTER.

A basic text page loaded. It was titled the Hidden Wiki. A catalog of the Dark Web's main resources, arranged by category. Some of the links caught Sokolov's eye.

```
Boys and Girls

Contract Killers

Black Market

Wallet Laundry

Guns and Ammo

Drug Store

PaedoParadise

Fake ID
```

Sokolov almost missed the exit off the highway. He followed the turn to Don Muang. As he approached the checkpoint, the armed guards let him through without inspection, seeing Kinkladze's embassy car. Once he parked the Toyota, Sokolov stayed inside, unable to take his eyes off the tablet's screen.

Designed with complete privacy in mind, the tablet's settings omitted browsing history and website cache. Sokolov had no way of finding Kinkladze's mailbox unless he knew the appropriate anonymous link.

But he could find something else. He tapped on the address marked *HiddenSearch*.

A plain search box came up. He entered his own name.

Eugene Sokolov.

SEARCH.

Pages upon pages of hits.

With bated breath, he opened a link.

```
Billionaire Bloodbout Fighting Tournament
```

`Venue: Billionaire Island Hotel and Casino`

Billionaire Bloodbout. Sokolov had never heard of such a contest before. He hadn't the slightest clue about Billionaire Island, either. Yet he found his name listed among the participants.

17

Sokolov headed for General Udomkul's office. Inside the handbag, he carried the tablet, casino chip, false passport and two bundles of cash.

He pictured the fate suffered by Alex Grib. Illicit bouts offered a quick buck for the less capable martial artists who knew no other trade. Especially so in Thailand, where the overall number of Muay Thai kickboxers measured in tens of thousands. Only a portion made it to the top with the skill level required for professional prize fighting. Thousands of others fell prey to a criminal industry from a young age. They ended up in matches that were absolutely brutal. Violence reigned supreme, fueling crowd instincts and underhand gambling. The fighters were expendable. The flow of new amateurs never ebbed. They came from Thailand's poorest rural areas, having no other means to survive. It was the rock-bottom level of illegal fighting. The ruthlessness differed little as one ascended. All that changed was the greater ability of fighters who competed for higher stakes. It came as no surprise to Sokolov that a disgraced outcast like Alex would be drawn to the shadier side of combat sports. His pedigree should have propelled him straight to the elite level of underground bouts, the razor edge where fortunes awaited on one side and death on the other. A high-risk tournament must have taken place at a nearby island, and Alex had entered it under Sokolov's name. That much seemed clear to him, and the rest didn't matter. Several hours later, his plane would touch down back in Moscow.

A helmeted guard ushered him into the general's office.

Greeting him, General Udomkul gestured at a lone metal chair across his desk. The general's workspace displayed typical paraphernalia: pens, papers, plastic models of jet fighters, a corded phone, a framed photo of His Majesty, the King of

Thailand.

"Please, take a seat, Major Sokolov."

Sokolov did.

"Thank you for your hospitality, General. I'm afraid it's time for me and my crew to leave. I trust everything is ready for our departure."

"Where's Mr. David?" the general asked bluntly.

"Mr. David will not be joining us at this moment. Regrettably."

General Udomkul scrutinized the bag.

"I'm so sorry. No problem. Mr. David and I had an arrangement that I'm sure you'll respect."

"Of course I will, if you remind me of the details."

"For every person leaving the airbase, a small fee must be paid." He scribbled a note and showed it to Sokolov.

$10,000.

"I'm sure there's a mistake."

Spittle flew from the general's mouth. "No mistake! Do you accuse me of lying?"

"By no means, General."

"You can call Mr. David and ask him." A yellow-toothed grin broke on the general's wrinkled, pockmarked face. He knew full well that Kinkladze was out of the equation.

Sokolov realized that he and his crew had become helpless, completely at the mercy of Udomkul. For certain, Kinkladze had agreed on a far more modest fee with the corrupt general. The twenty grand would have paid for a party of four: the three-man EMERCOM team and their passenger. Opportunistically, the general had now doubled his toll charges.

Sokolov had no way out. Udomkul effectively held the three of them hostage. One by one, he produced the ten-thousand-dollar bundles from the handbag and placed them on the general's desk.

Udomkul opened a drawer and put the cash away.

"Very good. But it's not enough."

"It's enough to secure safe passage for my pilots, Zubov and Mischenko."

"What about you?"

"I'll go back to Bangkok and bring you the money later."

"Oh, no. I can't allow you to return to Bangkok. It's very dangerous. The government is about to declare martial law. You should wait for Mr. David to come here and honor our agreement."

General Udomkul picked up the phone receiver from its cradle. "I'm calling the Russian embassy."

Sokolov depressed the switchhook. "That won't be necessary. I've got something else."

He produced the casino chip, holding the letter *B* in front of Udomkul's face.

The general's dark eyes glistened. His mouth creased. He set the receiver back in its cradle.

"Ah! Now we're talking."

"Do you know where it's from?"

Udomkul nodded soberly.

"Billionaire Casino. A private resort in the Andaman Sea."

"How much is the token worth?"

"A few thousand dollars."

"Here's the deal. You keep the token. I walk out, board my plane and fly away."

"Impossible. It's a sign of association with an exclusive club. Invitation-only, for men and women of immense power. An extremely lethal group of people. If my possession of such a token became known to them, they'd finish me."

General Udomkul pushed a button on the desktop phone base. A red light blinked.

"Your friends may go at once. But *you*, on the other hand ... you're nothing but a headache. I don't tolerate headaches. I get rid of them."

A trio of Thai soldiers stormed into the room, wielding Tavor TAR-21 assault rifles.

"You'll be taken to Billionaire Island. I'll let *them* deal with you. This way, I'll have nothing to worry about. And that's how you'll pay your fee."

The general cackled, his breath foul.

Holding Sokolov at gunpoint, the soldiers blindfolded and handcuffed him.

18

The soldiers led him away, prodding with their guns. Sweat rolled down his face underneath the grimy, oily rag which covered his eyes. He walked across the tarmac to a growing whine of helicopter engines. The pitch of the engine noise was unmistakable. He would recognize the sound of a Russian-made Mil Mi-17 under any circumstances.

The soldiers shoved him inside.

Disoriented inside the helicopter, Sokolov lost track of time. An hour must have passed. More than an hour. The Mi-17 was flying over sea.

Descent. At any moment, he expected the soldiers to open a hatch and drop him into the Gulf of Thailand. He would either crash against the water surface or drown.

Just as Alex had fallen to his death.

The realization scalded him. He started praying. He didn't care whether he was about die. He only thought about his friends. He prayed that Udomkul had kept his promise and let them go.

The helicopter landed. Sokolov shuffled his feet as he was pushed forward. Gruff voices swore at him in Thai. The soldiers threw him into the back of a truck. The rough road poked him with every bump. Finally, the truck stopped at a pier.

An excruciating motorboat journey followed. He felt the spray of water on his skin. With every passing second, he anticipated getting tossed overboard. A half hour later everything ended.

The boat moored at a different pier.

The soldiers handed him over to a group of guards waiting on the other side. He didn't know how many had surrounded him. They conversed in English as they hustled him down a path.

"Who the hell is that?"

"Someone named Eugene Sokolov."
Laughter erupted.
"What, another one?"

PART II

1

CALIFORNIA

Tears rolled down the delicately chiseled face of Stacie Rose, Australian fashion model and designer, twenty-two years young. A mournful black blazer traced the lines of her slender body as she gracefully walked through the Serbian Cemetery in Colma, CA. Passing dense rows of tombstones, she located the one that bore the name of Marie Jordan. Her waist-length strawberry-blond hair cascading, she laid a bouquet of white roses and lilies. Her handwritten message in the accompanying card read: *In Loving Memory of My Dear Aunt. You will be Missed. From Stacie.*

She clutched the golden pendant hanging from her neck—Aunt Marie's gift for her tenth birthday. Like a breaking dam, sobs raked her uncontrollably. Trembling, she buried her face in her hands to mute her weeping.

A hand brushed against her shoulder.

Startled, she flinched and turned sharply.

Behind her was a rotund elderly man with thin white hair, wearing a black cassock with a massive golden crucifix. The Orthodox priest stood a head shorter than her perfect runway-modeling height. His plump face featured a gray goatee and a pair of brooding black eyes which studied her intently.

"I'm sorry for your loss," the man said in a heavy Russian accent. "But Marie, God's servant, is in a better place now. Thankfully, she had returned to the fold of the only true Church, the Russian Church, before the Lord claimed her soul."

Regaining composure, Stacie produced a handkerchief from her tiny purse and dabbed away the streaking tears from her cheeks.

The town of Colma was a necropolis, a cluster of different graveyards located on the San Francisco Peninsula against the backdrop of distant Santa Cruz foothills and jutting palm trees. Although nominally Serbian, the Orthodox cemetery in Colma acted as the final resting place for Eastern Christians of all denominations. Russian graves were the most common.

"I'm looking for Father Philemon," she said.

"It is I," replied the priest. "And what is your name, my child?"

"Stacie."

The priest's face lit up in recognition, as though he'd long expected to see her.

"Stacie Rose. *Anastacia.*"

"*Da.*"

Something churned inside her at the mention of her Russian name. Anastacia was the only name Marie had called her, and Russian the only language they had conversed in, developing a special bond. She still remembered the language after so many years.

"It's such a shame that you couldn't attend the service yesterday," Father Philemon continued in Russian.

She lowered her eyes, unable to admit that she had barely scraped together enough money for the flight from Sydney, failing to do it in time. She was facing tough times as a freelance model and designer, but she preferred to keep her problems to herself. It was the price of her independence.

"What about your family?" he asked.

Stacie spoke Russian fluently, but with a soft Strine accent. "I lost my mom early and dad is now working in Africa as a doctor. We're hardly in touch. In truth, my dad never got along with Aunt Marie, even though she basically raised me before we moved to Australia. How did she die?"

Father Philemon let out a weary sigh.

"I don't know the details. But it was brutal. Someone broke into her house and stabbed her to death. Burglary. Some drug addict who completely lost his head, maybe. You'll have to ask the police. So terrible."

"If it *was* a burglar, do you know what he might have been looking for?"

Father Philemon shook his head.

"I'm not sure I understand," he replied uncertainly.

Stacie's eyes bored into his face.

"This is what I'll go to the police with. Three days before she died, Aunt Marie called me. She told me she had a document in her possession that she would give to *you* for safekeeping. A notebook. Its contents are extremely important. And according to her, I am the only person who has the key to the secret inside it. Now, Father Philemon, did she hand that notebook over to you or not? Pardon my language, but what the hell is going on?"

He stroked his beard pensively.

"I'm not sure how much of it your aunt told you, so I'll give you the whole story. It can be difficult to absorb all at once."

She noticed him staring at her bosom, but the priest immediately spared her the embarrassment of the situation.

"Anastacia, this necklace of yours. Do you know its meaning?"

Caught off guard by his real source of interest, she held the gold pendant. The elegant, medal-shaped surface was engraved with an elaborate design which had always intrigued her. A winged shield, adorned by a *fleur-de-lis* in the middle and a medieval knight helmet above it.

At one point, she had become obsessed with it, scouring every reference source she could get her hands on to find the symbol's origin. It was the obsession which had fueled her interest in art. Eventually, her search had faded away as she completed her Bachelor of Design degree.

"No, to this day it remains a mystery to me," she said. "It's similar to European emblems from the Middle Ages but nothing else matches it."

"In that case, I will reveal to you what it stands for," said Father Philemon. "It is the Oltersdorf family crest."

"Oltersdorf? I have never heard the name before," Stacie admitted. "Aunt Marie never mentioned it. And whenever I asked her, she always claimed she had no idea what the emblem meant, either."

"Believe me, Anastacia, she knew. She definitely did."

"It made no sense for her to lie to me. What does it have to do with her death, anyway?"

"Perhaps nothing. Given the current crime rate in San Francisco, I wouldn't be surprised if it turned out to be a tragic coincidence. She was, after all, an old lady living alone. But your pendant has everything to do with the reason she gave me the notebook you know of."

"And what might that be?"

In the most level voice possible, the priest said, "Just a small matter of two hundred million U.S. dollars."

"I'm sorry," said Stacie. "Did I hear right? You're talking about a fortune. What's that supposed to mean?"

"The Oltersdorf Estate. Two hundred million U.S. dollars in cash and gold deposits placed in banks around the globe. You may not be aware of the fact, but you have Oltersdorf blood in your veins. And that makes you the rightful heir to these assets."

Dumbfounded, Stacie just stood there for a few moments, catching her breath. The words staggered her. None of it could be true. The priest was mad.

Finally, she said, "Father Philemon, I have just lost my closest family member. If you're trying to kid me with such wild statements, you of all people, as a person of God, should know that it's not the time or place to do it."

"I understand your reaction. I would also be shocked by such bold claims. However, I'm absolutely serious about the words I choose, being one of the appointed executors of the Oltersdorf Estate—which is why Marie asked me for help."

"With all due respect, Holy Father, I still can't fathom ... I mean, it's a little overwhelming. An inheritance? All that money? Even if what you're saying is true, I can't possibly accept it. I don't want the burden—"

"That is something beyond your decision at the moment. There are rules, procedures, *protocols* that we must adhere to."

"What? I don't understand—"

"Let me explain everything from the very beginning."

"I'd appreciate that," she said in exasperation.

"The Oltersdorf nobility hails back to the thirteenth century, but I'm going to tell you about your great-great-grandfather. Baron Peter Oltersdorf was a general in the Russian Imperial Army throughout the First World War. He had a strong physical presence, an air of dignity and authority about him. I must say that your Oltersdorf roots are clearly evident, Anastacia. The fair hair, the fine aristocratic features, your graceful movement and stature. You have the piercing amethyst eyes of your great-great-grandfather. You even share the dimpled chin which is unmistakably Oltersdorf."

Feeling self-conscious, Stacie said, "I'll take that as a compliment, but it's Peter Oltersdorf I'd like to hear more about rather than myself."

The priest went on. "After the Revolution, he fought the Bolsheviks in Siberia. Sadly, the White Movement lost the civil war against the Reds. He was forced to flee to Manchuria with his family, alongside over one hundred thousand Russian refugees who flooded into the city of Harbin. Once there, the baron found himself in charge of considerable amounts of money remaining from his defeated army. A selfless man, the baron did his utmost to aid those Harbin Russians suffering the worst plight. But apart from his tireless work to help the Russian émigré community, he also harbored dreams of liberating Russia from the Bolshevik tyranny. He set up funds in Shanghai, Hong Kong, London, Japan and the U.S. to support his endeavor."

"Was there any chance of success?" Stacie asked, enthralled.

"That we will never know. The Second World War scuppered his valiant plans. The war broke out shortly after Oltersdorf began real action, sending small recon teams into Soviet territory— members of the Russian veterans organization which he headed. Eventually, he moved to Japanese-occupied Shanghai and then Japan proper. With no likelihood of leading the Russian liberation, his own future uncertain, and China most likely falling into communist hands, he made the only logical choice. The baron transferred what became known as the Oltersdorf fund into the trust of those who would continue the fight against Bolshevism until their beloved country was liberated. The Russian Orthodox Church Outside Russia."

"What happened to Peter Oltersdorf's family?"

"His wife passed away in the 1930s. During the war, his only daughter married a Cossack officer named Iordanov. She and her husband moved to the U.S. in 1945, where they changed their name to Jordan. They settled here in California and a few years later gave birth to their son, Jacob."

Stacie drew a sharp breath.

"Jacob Jordan."

"Your grandfather." The priest nodded. "He, of course, had two children: your Aunt Marie and Catherine, your mother. It took us quite a while to discover that."

"And the baron himself? My great-great-grandfather," she said with a measure of pride, now that her link to the Oltersdorf lineage felt tangible. "What became of him?"

"After the Japanese surrender, a Soviet SMERSH squad parachuted near Kyoto and captured Peter Oltersdorf in his residence. Without even a mock trial, they executed him."

"It's called murder," said Stacie.

"You could put it that way."

In her eyes, Father Philemon's story grew with believable detail, the initial claim no longer outlandish.

"Why is it only now that I've learned this about my family?"

"Like I said, the Church discovered your identity just a few days ago via your aunt. She contacted me to show me the personal notebook of Peter Oltersdorf. Like your pendant, it was given by him to his daughter, and passed on through generations. Following the baron's death, however, the Jordan family had kept the notebook's existence a secret, as well as their relation to the Oltersdorf bloodline."

"For what reason?"

"Maybe the family history was still too painful for them. Or perhaps they were waiting for the right time. As long as the communist threat existed, they might have feared retribution from Soviet agents. The Reds knew that Peter Oltersdorf had a daughter. Hunting for her father's secrets, it wasn't beyond them to track her down and use force against her family, even on U.S. soil. Until they felt safe, your grandparents chose to keep a low profile. I wouldn't blame them."

"So what made Aunt Marie give you the notebook?"

"I hate to say it, Anastacia, but she was an old woman in poor health. She wanted someone else to continue the Oltersdorf legacy, and wanted to pass it on before her time came. And she did. God works in mysterious ways." Father Philemon crossed himself emphatically.

Stacie's eyes reddened as she glanced at her aunt's grave.

"I still don't understand why, besides the notebook, I've inherited that staggering amount of money."

"The baron transferred his substantial funds to the Church on the condition that the resources be used exclusively to combat the communist regime until its fall and total destruction in Russia. However, the Soviet Union ceased to exist in 1991. The baron's wish fulfilled, there is nothing to fight against as such. Under the terms of the Oltersdorf Estate, the funds cannot be touched and must be provided to an Oltersdorf descendant for further disposition. The money hasn't been used since. Interest accrued."

"I guess a few unknown relatives could claim a stake in the two-hundred-million fortune. Why me?"

"Your aunt had no next-of-kin apart from you. We've run checks. Trust me, you are the sole descendant. The only Oltersdorf empowered to make the decision is the owner of the notebook. Besides, there's a catch. Peter Oltersdorf did not care for personal wealth, and he expected his offspring to follow his Christian virtue. The two hundred million will not belong to you directly, you will have to choose a charitable cause to spend it on. It is not so much an inheritance as an appointment. Your late Aunt Marie told me that you have a kind heart. I believe her. From now on, it is you who must run the Oltersdorf Estate and ensure that the funds are used appropriately. You have been chosen by God. I am merely serving as an instrument of His will." Father Philemon paused. "So, now you've heard the story. I can only pray that I've convinced you."

"If your sermons are half as convincing, you should have no shortage of converts," she said. "I'm still coming to terms with the whirlwind change suddenly going on in my life. I trust you, but this new reality is indeed difficult to cope with. And I feel I've barely scratched the surface, there's so much else I need to learn."

"You'll manage fine. Don't worry, someone else will fill you in on the details, especially the legal aspects. Father Mark from Hong Kong is more familiar with the finances, given that the Hong Kong banks are the ones where the main Oltersdorf accounts have been kept. He's eager to meet you. Father Mark is currently on a pilgrimage here, in San Francisco. I can introduce you right away if you don't mind a short drive."

"Wait," said Stacie. "First, I want to see Peter Oltersdorf's notebook. It was Aunt Marie's wish that I should receive it."

"Come with me and I'll show it to you. You may be able to uncover its secret."

2

They exited the cemetery. Father Philemon kept his car parked on the other side of the hedge-lined Hillside Boulevard. He pushed a button on his car key. A latest-model, obsidian-black Mercedes S600 winked twice in return.

"Wow, *this* is your ride?" Stacie said, surprised. "So much for taking a vow of poverty, I guess."

"It's not for luxury but ease of travel," the priest replied sternly. "I shun earthly riches. The vehicle is Church property."

"I'm sorry, I didn't mean to be rude."

"No offense taken," said Father Philemon as he held the passenger door open for her. "It's an age-old dilemma. As Archbishop, I must uphold a certain standing within the Russian community."

Throughout the quick drive to San Francisco, Stacie wondered what lay ahead for her. From barely scraping enough pocket change for an air ticket to potentially managing $200,000,000 was a big jump for anyone. Was it really happening? She considered the responsibility that went hand in hand with such a crazy amount of money. Would the burden crush her? Was she committing another mistake?

If God existed, Stacie thought, today's events manifested His Providence. It was Him she now trusted to guide her.

Her rebellious spirit had drawn her to the fashion world, only for her to realize that the glamor was fake. But hadn't she dreamed of gracing every magazine cover for the sole purpose of making a difference? She had envisaged herself as a goodwill ambassador once she'd reached fame, raising money for impoverished children. The Oltersdorf Estate would grant her that chance. Freedom came with responsibility, not the lack of it.

She could start her own charity. Devote herself to a worthy cause. Make amends and help her father's humanitarian effort in

Africa.

What if she failed? She had to try. No matter what, she knew she had nothing to lose.

She couldn't just turn her back on Aunt Marie's last wish and walk away.

At the very least, her duty was to preserve the baron's notebook.

She pushed the Oltersdorf Estate to the back of her mind.

Heading north-west through Golden Gate Park to Richmond District, the Mercedes turned onto Geary Boulevard.

As it suddenly came into view, Stacie faced the enormous white edifice of the Russian church. Its tall golden cupola shimmered brightly, reaching about a hundred feet in height. Four smaller turrets, crowned by onion domes, surrounded it. The curved-top façade was dominated by a gigantic eight-pointed Orthodox cross, flanked on either side by colorful murals depicting various Christian saints.

Above the massive wooden entrance, an ornate mosaic showed the Holy Mother of God with Her arms open in loving consolation to all who suffered.

"The Holy Virgin Cathedral," Father Philemon announced. "It was founded in 1961 by St. John of Shanghai and San Francisco."

"A modern-day saint?"

"Decades after his death, the body inside his sepulcher was found undecayed as proof of holiness. The incorrupt relics are now housed in a shrine inside the very cathedral he built. Truly, he was St. John the Miracleworker. An outstanding missionary and philanthropist. Like your great-great-grandfather, he was forced out of Russia by the Reds. From Belgrade, where he'd become a priest, he went to Shanghai. He had no bed because he hardly slept, either running the parish, working on his theological writings, holding services or visiting those who needed him. The power of his prayer was such that he healed even the hopelessly sick. Everybody who'd known him spoke of the divine grace he exuded. He radiated God's love for everyone, regardless of their denomination, and especially children. He set up orphanages, saving kids from the slums of Shanghai. After the Second World War, with the communist takeover of China imminent, he helped thousands of Russian refugees immigrate to the States. Also, St. John was a clairvoyant, even predicting the time and place of his own death in 1966."

"How I wish that such fascinating people were still around. The world needs someone like St. John."

Someone who isn't bothered whether a car brand reflects his social status, she almost added but thought better of it.

Father Philemon left the Mercedes at the curb in front of the cathedral. Stacie followed him toward the gold-painted entry door which he pulled ajar.

"The cathedral is open to the public only for religious service. Nobody will trouble us. Please, Anastacia, you must cover your head."

She pulled the silk scarf from her neck and draped it over her dazzling hair.

He ushered her inside. Stacie's heels clicked against the hardwood floor, the sound echoing softly around the cavernous space.

Stunned by the sight before her, she stood mesmerized. Her eyes had never before feasted on a scene quite as magnificent. It was as though she had stepped right into the middle of the New Testament. Glorious frescoes covered every inch of the Cathedral's walls. Vividly, the amazing interior came alive with biblical stories of Jesus Christ, the Virgin Mary, the Apostles, saints and angels, all painted by a hand so masterful that it could belong in the Louvre. With the ceiling converging almost sixty feet above her, the artistic panorama seemed to soar endlessly into the sky, enveloping Stacie.

The beauty of the paintings took her breath away. Her tears flowed silently. The gilded splendor of the iconostasis highlighted the Cathedral's richness. Five tiered chandeliers hung suspended under the cupolas, dwarfed by the surroundings full of divine imagery.

"Come along." Father Philemon took her by the arm and walked her across the nave, or the main part of the Cathedral. The correct word somehow popped up from the recesses of her memory, making Stacie appreciate her Architecture course and the church layout terminology it had included.

The entire nave was empty, the lack of pews rendering the area even more spacious. From silver-framed icons, haloed faces peered at her with mercy. To her right, she glimpsed the tomb of St. John of Shanghai and San Francisco.

Emerging from behind the iconostasis, a man stepped out onto the elevated ambo, a semicircular platform from which the priest delivers a sermon.

Of average height, the man wore a drab gray business suit and tie. He had a lantern-jawed face, short ginger hair and a Van Dyke beard.

"Father Mark!" called Philemon, approaching the man. "I'd like to introduce you to Stacie Rose."

"Father Mark?" she echoed. "You're a priest?"

"I am, indeed," the man replied. "Don't mind my civilian attire. I don't usually sport a cassock when I'm away from my parish. I'm a long way out from Hong Kong at Father Philemon's request, although I'm not here to conduct a service."

"Oh, I see," said Stacie.

"Now that you've cleared up the confusion, Father Mark, it's time to show Anastacia the object which has brought us all here together."

"It's hidden in the Sanctuary, exactly where you left it."

Father Philemon turned to Stacie. "Excuse me for a moment, but women aren't allowed anywhere near the altar. I'll be back shortly."

He proceeded through the Royal Gates and disappeared behind a curtain into the Sanctuary.

Stacie stayed behind with Father Mark. The spellbinding effect which the opulent décor had on her was yet to wear off, so it was the businesslike priest who broke the silence.

"I trust that Father Philemon has already acquainted you with the Oltersdorf Estate."

"He has, but I think I have more questions than answers right now."

"That was to be expected. You'll gain confidence once you've traveled to Hong Kong and familiarized yourself with the entire—"

"You want me to travel to *Hong Kong*?"

"Of course. You need some first-hand information in order to operate the funds."

Before Stacie could reply, Father Philemon returned, holding a leather-bound book in his hands. He proffered it to Stacie. She took the brown notebook with icy fingertips.

The texture of worn leather felt soft and crinkly to the touch. In shape and size, it was not at all dissimilar to the Moleskine notebooks of the early 20th century, favored by the likes of Picasso and Matisse. Instead of an elastic band, however, the pages were held closed by a length of string sealed with hot wax.

She examined the seal. The insignia imprinted in the red wax matched the emblem on her pendant; a winged shield, adorned by a *fleur-de-lis* in the middle and a medieval knight helmet above it. The Oltersdorf crest.

"Have you seen a similar notebook before?" asked Father Philemon.

"No, never."

"Are you certain?"

"Absolutely."

"Would you like to open it?"

"Yes, but ... I'd break the seal."

"It has stayed intact all these years just for you. The notebook *is* rightfully yours, Anastacia. By all means, do it. Your aunt wanted you to uncover its contents."

With great care, she pried open the sealing wax, her fingers trembling slightly. She didn't want to pulverize it. A piece broke off. She removed the seal and the piece of string, and placed both tenderly in her purse.

Holding her breath, she opened the thick cover and flipped the first couple of pages. Her great-great-grandfather's beautiful handwriting flowed across the yellowed paper. Strong yet elegant strokes of Cyrillic script. Stacie's heart sank.

"I don't understand," she murmured.

The problem wasn't that she'd forgotten written Russian. She could read the language and comprehend it proficiently. Yet the neatly-jotted words were not written in Russian at all. In fact, the text did not seem to be written in any language she recognized. It was ...

"Gibberish," she said, crushed by disappointment. "Is it Old Russian? Church Slavonic?"

She showed them the pages.

"It's definitely neither Church Slavonic nor Ancient Russian," said Father Philemon, shaking his head.

"But it's Russian all the same," said Father Mark. "Only it's written in code."

"Code?" Stacie repeated, her curiosity piqued.

"Some sort of cipher, definitely. Russian czars and noblemen sometimes used to write letters in such fashion."

"Do you know which cipher *this* is?"

"No. At least, not yet. I'm sure we'll learn the meaning from Peter Oltersdorf's papers, his personal archive stored in Hong Kong."

She looked up from the notebook at the red-haired priest sharply.

"Father Mark, you've mentioned going there."

"Any time, at a moment's notice. I arrived here on a private plane which is waiting at the airport. We can fly today if you have your passport with you."

3

After all, what harm could there be in flying to Hong Kong? Such was Stacie's frame of mind on her way to San Francisco International Airport. She had no business more pressing than dealing with the Oltersdorf Estate. She also hoped to find the answer to the mystery of the notebook which she held tightly in her hands.

However, why had Aunt Marie told her that Stacie possessed the key to its secret? The question nagged her.

The Mercedes reached the airport, located on the edge of the San Francisco Bay. From a design standpoint, the renovated terminals incorporated sleek, modern esthetics. Additionally functioning as a cultural gateway to the city, San Francisco International accommodated a museum, library, aquarium and live music events under its roof. She had arrived via Terminal 1 at 9 o'clock on that very same morning, after a grueling thirteen-and-a-half-hour economy-class flight. The flight to Hong Kong took fifteen hours, but Father Mark had promised it would be a much more comfortable experience.

She saw what he meant as Father Philemon parked the Mercedes in a special lot just outside the executive terminal and led her and Father Mark into the lush private lounge. In contrast to the body searches, check-in lines and long layovers of airline travel, Stacie enjoyed the VIP treatment as she sank into a cozy sofa. A receptionist called up the plane's pilots. A few minutes later, their business jet pulled up on the tarmac, ready for boarding. Stacie followed the priests out onto the runway to the waiting aircraft. The twin-engine plane was arrow-sleek, from its oval-shaped fuselage to the winglets projecting from the tips of its wings.

"After you, Baroness Oltersdorf," said Father Mark. Stacie's cheeks flushed scarlet.

She climbed up the stairs, greeted by one of the two pilots.

"Welcome aboard the Gulfstream G650," said the uniformed, clean-shaved crew member, "the finest aircraft available for your comfort. Please take any seat you fancy."

Her choice was abundant. She proceeded into the sizable cabin where four pairs of huge chairs stood facing each other, providing ample legroom. First-class sophistication shone through every detail of the interior. Cream-colored fabric lined the main seating area. The quality of materials and craftsmanship impressed her, with custom-tailored silk carpets, glossy wooden finishes and brushed metal fittings employed throughout. As she reclined in a chair, she appreciated the suppleness of the hand-stitched leather upholstery. Father Mark occupied the opposite chair and Father Philemon took the seat behind her.

The Gulfstream taxied out on the runway and took off effortlessly. As the jet gained altitude, a splendid view of the northern Bay opened through the extra-large windows, including a glimpse of the Golden Gate Bridge.

No sooner had the plane finished its buttery-smooth climb than Father Mark got out of his chair and loomed over Stacie.

"I bet all that flying must be pretty tiresome. You could use some sleep right now."

"I do feel a little exhausted," she said, "but I'm too pumped up—"

Fiercely, without warning, Father Mark pinned her wrists down against the chair.

"What the hell are you doing?" she shouted.

"Trapping a dumb girl!" he snarled, his hold unrelenting.

She screamed in terror, twisting and kicking. A wet piece of cloth pressed to her face muffled her helpless cry as Father Philemon grabbed her throat from behind. She stopped struggling, her limbs going numb as she sucked air through the pungent-smelling rag. Her vision blurred and she could no longer hear her own suppressed whimper. The last thing her mind registered before slipping into the chloroform-induced oblivion was Father Mark ripping the golden pendant off her neck.

4

"Now then, can anyone tell me who this is?"

In the dimly lit auditorium, Constantine Sokolov engaged the nineteen freshmen who attended his Russian History class. Controlling the classroom projector from his phone, Constantine brought up a photo onto the screen. It was an aged black-and-white portrait of a Soviet general in uniform. Rows of medals decorated his chest. His dark slicked-back hair revealed a low forehead and a flat, round face set in a stony expression, his thin lips taut. His hard, leery stare added to the no-nonsense appearance.

"Any ideas?" he prodded the students to participate.

Lydia, a freckled, bespectacled girl, raised her hand. "A veteran?"

"Must be a war hero!" called out a turtleneck-wearing kid named Vlad.

"Very good. You're almost correct, but not quite. This man's name is Vasili Blokhin, and he was a record-breaking mass murderer. As Stalin's chief executioner, he killed up to *fifty thousand* people *himself.*"

A murmur of voices undulated in response: *"No way... Wow ... My God ...!"*

Constantine flicked the next PowerPoint slide, which displayed a shocking image. Rows of exhumed corpses lined the ground. A caption read: *THE KATYN MASSACRE, 1940.*

"In his most horrifying feat, Blokhin carried out the extermination of the Polish military elite. Out of the twenty thousand captive officers slaughtered in the Katyn massacre, Blokhin shot seven thousand with his own hand. The carnage went on for twenty-eight days. He and his henchmen killed the prisoners in ten-hour shifts. Blokhin murdered 250 people each night, at a rate of one man every two and a half minutes."

Constantine swiped the screen back to the portrait photograph.

"You can see here that one of the medals he's wearing is the Order of the Red Banner, the highest Soviet military decoration. Stalin awarded it to him in October, 1940, specifically for the Katyn massacre. Blokhin retired in 1953 after three decades of *irreproachable service*, as noted in the citation celebrating his career. He never answered for his crimes. He also received the Order of the Patriotic War, making him officially a veteran of the Second World War." Constantine added sardonically, "Next time when you see a teary-eyed Soviet war survivor being thanked on Red Square, he might be a former member of an NKVD death squad."

He switched off the projector and turned up the lighting.

"Vasili Blokhin is a vivid example of the system of total oppression set up by the Bolsheviks. As seen from the British report which I showed you last week, the civilized world knew about it from the very beginning. The Bolsheviks *institutionalized* evil. Modern Poland has stood up for its fallen officers, demanding answers. But what of Russia? The likes of Blokhin numbered in the thousands. How many massacres did they orchestrate against *Russian* officers, peasants, clergy, workers, the entire nation?" he asked rhetorically. "What I call a *kakistocracy*, the rule of the worst, resulted from this sort of negative selection. Perhaps even more devastating than the physical genocide of Red Terror was the moral corruption it entailed. Paranoia, deception, treachery, hypocrisy, fear, betrayal, bribery, spying, theft, envy and hatred all permeated the Soviet society from top to bottom. The long-lasting effects of such degradation are evident to this day. Almost every problem challenging us has Stalinist roots."

He glanced at his watch. He was running out of time. Ending the lecture, he told them which chapter to read for the next class.

Constantine collected his notes and stepped outside the auditorium.

Bad news awaited him in the shape of Sarah Lvovna, Dean of the History Department. In an unfortunate turn of events, she happened to be his boss at RSHT College. A loyal *apparatchik*, she had hired him only because of a severe staff shortage and couldn't wait to kick him out at the end of the semester. His qualifications could have earned him a teaching position at Moscow University. Yet due to political pressure, every institution in town had shunned him, barring the impossibly acronymed, third-rate school where he made a living as an adjunct professor. Not that the younger female contingent minded that he'd ended up at their college. Postgrad girls flocked around him, using every opportunity to flirt with the tall, fit, charming, sandy-haired teacher with brooding eyes who was still in his thirties. He enjoyed the fleeting romantic affairs, so the job carried a few bonuses. But above all, he took earnest satisfaction in educating freshmen. He was going to stick around for a while. But his time was really running out, if the dean's glare was any indication.

In lieu of makeup, Sarah Lvovna's face wore a perpetual scowl. She kept her rat's nest of hair knotted in a messy bun. She was always dressed in a colorless calf-length skirt which matched a faded sweater, reeking of stale perfume. He had no clue about her age, but she looked older than Lenin and twice as scary.

"Young man, what is the meaning of this? Your conduct is outrageous!"

"How outrageous?" he inquired.

"I'll have none of your cheek. I've heard of your so-called lecture, everything you said! It's pure anti-Soviet propaganda. Our job is to foster patriotism!"

"My job is to teach history."

Ignoring him, she said, "You're smearing our country's Soviet past. The greatest period when America feared us! The Russian society must stand united. Instead, you are subverting the youth, violating every educational policy and undermining national interests. Tell me, Sokolov, why do you hate Russia so much?"

"The Soviet Union isn't Russia. It's the antithesis of Russia. The anti-Russia."

Sarah Lvovna's eyes bulged furiously. "This is scandalous! You're a traitor to your Soviet motherland!"

"I'm sorry, define *Soviet*?"

"What?!" The old woman gaped at him, fuming.

"You heard me. What's the meaning of the word 'Soviet'? A *soviet* was a socialist representative organ. Do you realize that the Bolsheviks named their republic after a *bureaucracy*? The Soviet Union had nothing to do with Russia apart from seizing her territory and resources. To quote the Russian philosopher Ivan Ilyin, *Soviet patriotism* is allegiance to the government and not the country, to the regime and not the people, to the party and not the homeland. Anyone claiming that the Soviet Union was a Russian national state is either a fool or a liar."

"How dare you?" the dean shrieked. "How dare you! Sokolov, consider your contract terminated with immediate effect!"

He chuckled. "Make that by mutual consent, then. Goodbye."

He stormed off, leaving her in his wake.

"Oh no, you're not getting off that easy!" she shouted from the far end of the linoleum-floored corridor. "I'll report your revisionist views to the authorities! You'll rot in prison for anti-government activity and extremism!"

"How very Soviet of you."

Constantine took the stairway to the ground floor, where he got the coat-check attendant to fetch his warm jacket. Putting it on, he strode out of the college building, never to return.

That was it, then: he'd become virtually unemployed again. He might have held his temper in check, but the dean would have fired him regardless of his attitude. That old Stalinist hag hated his guts. She had been picking her chance to confront him, his academic fate already sealed. To hell with it. He didn't worry about leaving his students like Vlad or Lydia. He'd developed their talent for critical analysis. The rest was up to them. You couldn't teach independent thought—or smother it.

He shivered from the biting wind at a lamppost-illuminated bus stop. It was only 5 p.m., but the winter sky had already darkened to pitch black after sunset. Icy gusts billowed snow at his feet. The northern climate depressed him. He reached for the phone to call his younger brother. He had failed to get in touch with Eugene for a couple of days now. He hit speed dial once more, with growing concern.

Again, the call went straight to voicemail.

Gene, where the hell are you?

5

Eugene Sokolov had spent the last several hours locked up inside a metal cage contained within in a windowless wooden shed. The cage was no larger than a phone booth. The steel bars of the cage, linked by mesh, were invulnerable. He had been stripped to his underwear and given no food or water. The only available amenities included a bright light bulb hanging from the ceiling and a hole in the floor for his bodily functions.

The door remained closed. No guards entered to check on him. He'd yelled at the wooden walls of the shed, to no avail. Rage had turned to desperation, tedium, then numbness. In the cramped space, he couldn't lie down, sit or even crouch. Perspiration slicked his skin. Heat and humidity built up within the confines of the narrow shed. The standing cell where he found himself imprisoned had been fashioned as a sweatbox. Incarceration itself became torture. He was suffocating from the stuffy, foul air. Energy was sapped from his body. His every muscle and joint hurt from the incessant punishment of his physical position. Instead of sleep, he drifted in and out of semi-consciousness. Disoriented, he'd lost all track of time.

Through the seemingly-infinite stupor, his sharp hearing picked up a sound. The bolt of the wooden door creaked and it swung open.

A pair soldiers, AKs slung over their shoulders, splashed bucketfuls of ice-cold water into the cage. The shock cut Sokolov's breath short.

The soldiers unlocked the cage and shoved him outside the shed. Holding him at gunpoint, they motioned for him to move forward. He gulped the fresh air, trudging along a footpath through tropical undergrowth.

His senses were slowly recovering from the claustrophobic confinement. As he cleared the shrubbery, he struggled to fully appreciate the scenic view of Billionaire Island. Turquoise waves lapped the pristine, crescent-shaped beach. The sandy coastline curved around a bay, separated by a coral reef from the sapphire-blue mass of the Andaman Sea beyond. Palm trees swayed in the gentle breeze, offering shade from the scorching sun.

The warm sand soothed his bare feet. He scanned the shore. The unspoiled landscape offered no means of escape. He lacked the strength to mount a resistance and he had nowhere to run. Knowing it, the two soldiers took their convoy duty with slackened discipline. Along the way, they chewed the mildly narcotic khat leaves which hued their teeth vampire-red. As far as he could tell, their uniforms identified them as Burmese infantrymen. They encountered a group of three other Burmese soldiers patrolling the beach, who exchanged jokes with Sokolov's escorts, no doubt at his expense.

Up ahead, he saw a sprawling palatial structure with a multi-tiered roof, reminiscent of a Thai royal residence. Preceding it was a row of smaller villas built in similar style. Each white-walled villa had a private infinity pool stretching from its sun terrace. For some reason, the guards were leading Sokolov to the nearest villa. He had no idea what his captors might want from him. The swinging polarity of the prisoner's condition was a common interrogation tactic. Whatever they were going to do to him, he'd rather they did it inside a luxury villa than a cage in a jungle shed. Swiping the card-key, one soldier held the door open, and the other thrust the barrel of his AK at Sokolov in a less-than-jovial invitation to enter.

As if transported from hell to paradise, Sokolov crossed the threshold. The door slammed shut behind him. He was welcomed by a cool blast from the air-conditioner. Padding across the marble floor, he inspected the house. The spacious rooms were interconnected by archways. A glass wall separated the living room from an indoor spa area, overlooking the sea. A giant Jacuzzi was built into the teak decking. He slid a panel open, slipped inside and immersed himself in the water.

Soaking in the tub, he lathered his skin with lemongrass-fragranced shampoo, scrubbing away the grime. It felt like the most refreshing bath he'd ever taken. Toweling, he became aware of his complete nakedness. He found no bathrobe or a single item of clothing apart from a *gi* kimono and pants hanging in the bedroom wardrobe. The karate *gi* outfit was not unlike those he owned. The *gi* came with a pair of Japanese wooden flip-flops called *geta*, and there was no kind of other footwear in sight. Reluctantly, he put the whole costume on.

Odder still, he discovered two objects left for him atop the perfectly-made king-size bed. One was his Breitling Superocean chronometer. The dial showed that he'd stayed inside the shed for thirty-six hours. Had someone tampered with the date on his watch, pranking him? Or had he actually remained locked in that cage for a day and a half? His captor showed a dark sense of humor in either case. The second object was his Russian passport, which had Alex Grib's mugshot stapled over his own. Very funny, Sokolov thought mirthlessly. He clasped the Breitling's familiar bracelet on his wrist and hid the passport in a fold of the *gi*.

Returning to the front door, he twisted the knob but it was locked. Outside, the Burmese soldiers guarded the villa. He was a detainee all the same, despite the upgrade of prison conditions, and even that seemed temporary. He proceeded to the dining room, allured by a savory aroma of food wafting from within.

The massive dining table was stacked with enough dishes to fill the menu of an Asian restaurant. Steaming bowls of tom yum soup and fried rice, assorted platefuls of dim sum, chicken curry, shrimp rolls, and chili crab were the most tantalizing among others, topped off by a fruit platter of papaya, mango, yellow-flesh watermelon, and red bananas.

He resisted the urge to jump at the table and devour all the food at once. Gorging might make him throw up. Contrary to what his stomach told him, he poured himself a glass of pineapple juice and sipped it carefully. There were no utensils on the table apart from a set of ivory chopsticks. A knife, fork or spoon were deemed too dangerous in his hands. Deftly using the chopsticks, he ate a small portion of vegetable fried rice.

Suddenly, he heard a knock at the front door. The show of courtesy amused him. Was he supposed to rush to the door and ask his visitors inside? He wiped the corners of his mouth with a silk napkin, leaving the table just as the unexpected guest entered the villa.

Unexpected was an understatement—it was the last person he'd hoped to see.

"*You?*"

"Well, well, Major Sokolov. We meet again!"

The elderly man, well into his seventies, had the wrinkled face of a Shar-Pei, with a bulbous nose ridden with broken capillaries, puffy eyes and the stare of a dead fish. It was a face Sokolov had seen numerous times on TV and in person. Saveliy Ignatievich Frolov, former head of the KGB Fifth Chief Directorate, former Director of the FSB, paced the marble floor, nodding approvingly at the rich furnishings. Uncharacteristically, in lieu of a gray suit, Frolov was dressed in a flowery shirt, Bermuda shorts, and sandals which he wore over black socks.

"No offer of a handshake, I see," said Frolov. "Understandable, really. Mind if I join you for lunch?"

"Be my guest."

"Ah, thank you, Eugene."

Frolov followed him back into the dining room and immediately helped himself to a pile of minced pork noodles.

"What the hell are you doing here?" Sokolov asked, eying the old man with disdain.

"Lots of retired KGB officers have settled in Thailand, didn't you know? I happen to own a bungalow in Pattaya. Not as ritzy as this villa, of course, but I'm a man of modest needs. So I just wanted to drop by as soon as I learned that you got involved in our operation."

"So you're the one running this little show here? But I thought that you were—"

"Finished? Gimme a break, Sokolov. You didn't actually think that just because your boss, Klimov, forced me to resign from my post, I would be down and out, did you? You're both not very bright, then. In a country where eighty percent of the government is run by former KGB men, how long could I stay out of a job, with my experience? Leaving my position of FSB Director wasn't some sort of fall from grace. Hell, it meant nothing. Heading the FSB wasn't even the highest status I attained in my life. I was once a candidate member of the Soviet Politburo. Everything else is a step down in comparison. I wielded so much power, your stupid Minister couldn't dream of —and I still do wield it. It's only that I'm now out of the spotlight as special adviser to the Kremlin."

"Advising them on what?"

"Religious affairs."

"How to sell one's soul to the devil?"

"You're far too bold and cheerful for a condemned man like yourself," said Frolov. "As a matter of fact, I'm Grand Commander of the Order of Holy Orthodox Knights."

"Sounds like a Masonic lodge."

Frolov swallowed a mouthful of noodles. "Like I said, its affiliation is Orthodox."

"Orthodox what? Orthodox Stalinism? Should be right up your alley."

"Fool, it's a non-profit organization that supports the cooperation between the Church and the Kremlin."

"Non-profit? Beggars belief. So, Grand Commander, was that priest one of your men?"

"He had to be eliminated, unfortunately. And the person running the show, as you phrased it, is Mr. Song. You may have seen him when he shot the priest. Billionaire Island is his domain: he's a god here, pardon the pun. The North Korean government put him in charge here, leasing the island from the Burmese."

"And Alex Grib? Eliminated like the priest? Did you also have a hand in killing him?"

"Alex punched above his weight, so to speak. Mr. Song hired him for the fighting tournament, a great source of entertainment for Song's guests. Somehow, Alex broke into Song's computer and stole valuable business information. He blackmailed Song, threatening to relay the information to the CIA. Huge mistake, as Alex soon learned, feeding the fish. You persist in being just as pesky. Song was going to send you to your doom, just as he dispatched your former friend. Only this time, your body would never be found." Frolov pushed away his plate. "Luckily for you, I dissuaded him. And I went to great lengths to get you from that cage to this lovely villa. There are only twelve guest villas on Billionaire Island, and each stay costs fifty thousand dollars per night. So you should be a little more appreciative of my concern."

"I'm practically weeping from such generosity. What gives?"

"Don't kid yourself, Eugene. You will die today, but your death will be a little more dignified. You see, Alex Grib's untimely demise has presented Song with a bit of a problem. His brawls were a huge attraction, not least because Alex claimed your pedigree as his own. However, now the man impersonating Eugene Sokolov is dead. So *you* will take his place in the Billionaire Bloodbout. The real Eugene Sokolov stepping in for the impostor, what a cruel twist."

Frolov reached across the table, handing Sokolov a rolled-up strip of thick, black cotton. Sokolov unwound it to see that it was an exact replica of his fourth-level black belt, complete with his name sewn in golden katakana.

"Fighting dressed as your own copy." Frolov smirked. "But you'll do it just once. I regret to inform you that you won't survive the Bloodbout, even if you manage to beat today's opponent. Once you enter the ring, you won't make it out alive. There will be no winner."

With that, Saveliy Frolov—former FSB Director, KGB Directorate Head, Politburo candidate and current Kremlin adviser on religion—rose from the table.

"Oh, and do try the spicy beef salad, it's delicious," he said, departing. "After all, this *is* your last meal."

6

Stacie Rose awoke to a killer headache, her mind hazy. She had been chloroformed repeatedly, parts of her memory blanked out. She found herself sprawled atop a bed in some sort of a boudoir. The room was dimly lit and colored in maroon and gold hues. She realized that her clothes were gone. In the ceiling mirror she saw that she was wearing nothing but a one-piece swimsuit. It was a black monokini which accentuated her curves with cut-out sides. The deep plunge revealed her navel.

She had no recollection of changing her clothes or ending up wherever she was. She was sickened by the mere thought that someone might have stripped her naked, made physical contact with her nude body, or worse ...

She touched her bare neck where the pendant should have been. The day's events came back in nightmarish fragments. The abduction aboard the Gulfstream. The repulsive stench of chloroform. The transfer to a different plane, an amphibian. A hypodermic needle piercing her skin. The airframe rattling as the plane rode foam-crested sea waves, plowing the teal water, taxiing to moor at a jetty. Father Philemon barking out orders to a trio of Asian soldiers who hauled her into the back of a metallic-painted SUV. The beach drive taking her to a palace with Burmese-style pyatthat roofs layered like umbrellas.

Her mind slid back into darkness ...

Father Philemon spearheaded the procession as the armed soldiers half-carried, half-jostled her across marble-floored halls and up a massive teak stairway. Stacie shuffled her feet groggily, stabs of pain piercing her liver with each step. On the top floor, she was brought to a carved teak door. Under the eye of a surveillance camera, Father Philemon banged on the wood with a gilded doorknocker. The lock clicked, the priest opened the door, and the soldiers tossed her on the hard padauk parquet. She landed awkwardly on her elbow, gritting her teeth from the pain and anger as she tried to pick herself up.

An Oriental man sitting behind an antique desk scrutinized her. He was dressed in a brilliant white tuxedo. His heterochromial glare was the most chilling she had ever experienced, the eyes soulless, full of predatory malice toward his defenseless prey. With a servile bow, Father Philemon approached him, set the Oltersdorf notebook on the desk and stepped back.

"Ms. Rose, I presume?" the Asian asked in English.

"Who are you? Is this some sort of a cult?" Her voice quivered. She had no idea what to expect from her kidnappers.

"You may call me Mr. Song. Unlike Father Philemon, I can't claim that I formally belong to any religion. I believe in no deity apart from our supreme leader, Kim Jong-Un."

She frowned. This was madness. She wouldn't have anything to do with North Korea! How did she get caught up in this mess?

"What do you *want* from me? Whatever it is that you're interested in, I know nothing beyond what *this* man told me," she said, referring to the priest.

Song flipped through the notebook.

"You're lying. A secret message is encrypted in this notebook. There is a *second* notebook—a codebook—which deciphers it. You *will* tell me where it is."

Her mouth felt dry. "*What*? You're mistaken. I've never heard about any such codebook."

"*Confess*!" hissed Song. "*You have the key*! It's in your best interests to give me the codebook or else you'll die suffering!"

"Anastacia hasn't yet realized the gravity of her situation," said Father Philemon.

Song laughed wickedly.

"She will, soon enough! She'll also realize she's inside the area known as the Golden Triangle. She's about to experience the meaning of the term in full. A few more injections, and she'll become a heroin addict. Then she'll *beg* to tell us everything we want to know."

In panic, Stacie gaped at the small bruise on her forearm.

7

Father Philemon steered the metallic Range Rover Sport along the turquoise edge of the Andaman Sea. The luxury SUV made for an excellent beach buggy, spewing sand from under its wheels, the four-wheel-drive managing the terrain effortlessly. Philemon was heading back toward the jetty, where a couple of identical seaplanes bobbed on the water surface.

"Are you sure you won't be staying for tonight's performance?" he asked his passenger.

"Unfortunately, no," Frolov replied. "I must return to Moscow without delay. It's a shame I won't get to witness Sokolov's death with my own eyes, but I have to oversee the final phase of Operation Temple."

"Mr. Song has promised to send you the full video of the Bloodbout via the Dark Web."

"I appreciate that. Give him my regards."

"And you, Saveliy Ignatievich, please pass along my greetings to His Holiness."

"I will. The Patriarch will be delighted to hear how you handled the Oltersdorf affair. It's game-changing. Speaking of the girl, you must break her as soon as possible. Use any means necessary. She's expendable, but make sure she gives up the location of the codebook before she dies."

"Anastacia can't tell us something she doesn't know. Father Mark believes he has a different lead. She may have given us the key unwittingly. The clue is in her pendant."

"That would be a major breakthrough. As a last resort, use brute-force decryption. Analyze the text for vulnerabilities. If Peter Oltersdorf made even a single error in his cipher, we must find it."

"Rest assured, we'll crack the code one way or another."

"You'd better. Otherwise the notebook is as useful as a doorstop. Don't forget, there's two hundred *billion* at stake. The odds will swing massively in our favor."

"Operation Temple is of paramount importance to the Moscow Patriarchate. I assure you that each of us will work tirelessly until we triumph. Nobody shall stand in our way now." The priest stopped the car. "Have a safe journey, Saveliy Ignatievich."

"Thank you, Father Philemon."

Frolov got out of the Range Rover and marched to the jetty.

8

SHANGHAI

Father Mark felt swelling excitement as the Gulfstream touched down in Shanghai and he took a chauffeured Mercedes to Xinle Road in Xuhui District. Should his hypothesis prove correct, it would propel his career to great heights. The Patriarchate was growing desperate for success in the Oltersdorf affair. And he would be the one to bring it.

Analytical thinking was a skill which he had developed decades before at the KGB spy school in Minsk. He also considered himself an adroit reader of human behavior. He preferred psychological rather than physical methods of coercion. Unlike Song, who only utilized brute force, Mark wasn't a sadist. Prior to his posting to Hong Kong, Mark had worked at a church in St. Petersburg, recruiting young radicals for a pro-Kremlin paramilitary group. He'd learned to crack body language, eye expressions and other nonverbal signals instantly. Anastacia Rose was an open book. From her stunned reaction, he could tell that the girl had been completely oblivious to the existence of the Oltersdorf codebook. The North Korean would torture her to death, without any result. Her fate didn't bother Mark, he only cared about achieving goals.

Again, he inspected the golden pendant. It *had* to be the key. The single object transferred to the girl by her aunt. Etched into the back of the pendant was the number: *1937.*

'Thirty-seven, the year of Stalin's Great Terror which had swept millions.

But 1937 also marked a different date which Father Mark was aware of.

As instructed, the Chinese chauffeur parked the car at Xinle Road, and Mark got out. Shanghai's Xuhui District had belonged to the French Concession in the 19th century, its boulevards almost Parisian in style. Once a premier residential district, it had been turned into a factory zone and subsequently redeveloped as the city's major commercial and shopping area.

Xinle was a narrow, low-rise lane of tightly-packed colonial buildings. Stores and cafés sprawled along the leisurely sidewalks, shaded by plane trees lining the street, still carrying the old-world romance of the French Concession.

At an intersection, an immense white edifice materialized from behind the trees. The glorious structure had been the Shanghai Orthodox Cathedral, its design fashioned after the destroyed Cathedral of Christ the Savior in Moscow. Today all that remained was a ghost of the church which St. John had built in *1937*.

St. John of Shanghai and San Francisco.

Two churches constructed under the supervision of St. John and the support and sponsorship of Peter Oltersdorf, together with the entire Russian community.

Two notebooks. One discovered in San Francisco. The other had to be in Shanghai. Inside the cathedral.

Former cathedral, Mark noted with a smirk. Since taking over, the Red Chinese had used it as a warehouse for twenty years, then converted it into a restaurant and nightclub, and later a part-time gallery.

A good place to eat according to fen shui, Mark mused cynically.

The restaurant still operated in the narthex—the western end of the cathedral—and the rest of the 35-meter-tall church building stayed shut down most days of the week. It opened to the public occasionally to display the works of local artists and otherwise stood neglected. The celestial domes had turned an eerie black. The Christian crosses had been toppled from the spires by the Chinese decades ago.

Mark entered through the main liturgical doorway on the eastern side. A uniformed Chinese guard shot him a bored look. The cavernous space of the church, capable to hold an attendance of 2,500 Christian worshipers, had been stripped bare, given a fresh coat of paint and divided by a maze of partitions. The partitions were burdened by evenly-spaced depictions of the Cultural Revolution hanging in massive frames. From his limited knowledge of Chinese he'd picked up in Hong Kong, Mark read a sign which identified it as an exhibition of Maoist art. Only a couple of indifferent visitors loitered.

Electric light blazed from a succession of chandeliers. His footsteps echoing as he crossed the stone floor, Mark paused in front of a Chairman Mao portrait, feigning interest. He glanced at the guard, who paid no heed to the Westerner in civilian attire. Mark knew he could roam the cathedral while drawing no suspicion.

Apart from its architecture, the interior was ideologically sterile, bearing no trace of its religious origin. Flower pots and trash cans occupied the alcoves meant for crosses and icons. Mark gathered his bearings and proceeded to the spot where the altar should have been. The whole area was as empty as the rest of the cathedral. There wasn't a nook and cranny to hide anything. Mark muttered a desperate curse under his breath. The last thing on his mind was accepting defeat and flying to Hong Kong empty-handed. He lifted his eyes and then he saw it.

Beneath the cupola was a mezzanine intended for the church choir. Glancing over his shoulder at the single guard, Mark slipped behind a partition which separated the area from the restaurant's backdoor. Next to it, he found a spiral staircase, sealed off with barrier rope. An attached sign read:

NO ADMITTANCE, CLOSED TO VISITORS.

The staircase led to the abandoned inner balcony. He pushed aside the stanchion and climbed up the stairs.

Dust billowed in the rays of light filtering from the cathedral's tall windows. Nobody had set foot on the mezzanine in years. Located at least fifteen meters above ground level, it offered a view of the entire cathedral floor below. Mark looked around the walls of the mezzanine. The ancient paint had cracked and crumbled. On the opposite wall across from the staircase, the underlying layer of paint revealed a ... No, not a fresco, Mark decided as he approached it. A faded emblem.

The Oltersdorf crest.

Mark knelt and produced a pocket knife, rapping the floor tiles with the handle, one by one.

He almost missed it. A hollow sound.

He rammed the blade under a loose tile and pried it open. It yielded a cavity in the floor. A secret cache.

There was an object inside. A satchel. With bated breath, Mark pulled it out and opened it.

It contained a notebook. Bound in black leather.

Even before he examined the wax seal, he knew that he'd found what he'd come for.

The Oltersdorf codebook.

9

The patrons had already filled the ornate hall of Billionaire Casino for the big mid-afternoon event. At the poolside entrance, Thai girls in floral bikinis welcomed a few tardy guests with trays of champagne. Several pricey hookers were lounging on the pool's sundeck with only the most minuscule slivers of fabric on their enticing bodies. Chatchai recognized a few of them. But it was a young woman he'd never seen before who made him stop cold. The only Caucasian, a beautifully proportioned blonde, she lay soaking up the sun in a strappy bathing suit. She was no call girl, that much was certain. She had too much class about her, which made her stand out from the flock of prostitutes. Even her swimwear looked like a luxury-brand item. But something else about her appearance had caught Chatchai's attention. He noticed needle marks and bruises on her right forearm. He didn't need his prior experience at the Narcotics Suppression Bureau to tell that she was stoned on drugs. The position of the bruising suggested that she had struggled as someone had injected her. She had no sunglasses on. Her eyelids were heavy, the gaze distant.

A cassock-clad Russian priest kept vigil next to her like a medieval sentinel. Catching his mad glare, Chatchai felt uneasy and proceeded inside.

Chatchai entered the casino and sat in front of a slot machine, the last unit in a row of blinking and jingling electronic contraptions. The position gave Chatchai an excellent view of the entire gaming area. Traditionally dressed Asian waitresses roamed between tables, serving drinks. Two distinct groups occupied the game tables: North Korean and Burmese delegations. Top-ranking military officials and their cohorts, aides, and civilian cronies. He recognized the ancient North Korean generals by their tan uniforms. The Burmese brass wore swamp-green tunics and their non-military associates were clothed in white shirts with skirt-like lungis.

Together, they had funneled billions off their oppressive regimes, milking their respective countries dry. Now they were throwing away that money at roulette, craps and blackjack tables. A single gaming chip could feed a starving Burmese or North Korean village. With stacks of chips being shuffled on the tables, the corrupt generals never seemed troubled by pangs of guilt, discussing deals with their counterparts.

Tension hung in the air despite the noise of loud conversation and occasional roars of laughter breaking out from different corners. Not one among the two dozen men inside the Casino had come here to try their luck at cards or dice. The stakes were much higher. Everybody was anticipating the Bloodbout. There was an atmosphere of growing excitement. Chatchai mopped his brow, perspiring despite the Casino's frosty air-conditioning. As he fed his last credit to the hungry slot machine, he stole a nervous glance at his watch.

ETA ten minutes. Chatchai swallowed. His own gamble had to pay off if he wanted to survive.

The main event was about to start shortly. Chatchai looked around the gilded interior of Billionaire Casino, rich with carvings, marble columns and golden statues, all worthy of decorating a royal palace. A presentation stage was situated at the far side of the hall, with a backdrop of three huge rear-projection screens.

As if on cue, epic cinematic music blared from the on-stage speakers. Fountains of sparks jetted in a grand pyrotechnic blast.

No sooner had the smoke cleared than Song appeared on the stage in a white tuxedo. All eyes turned to him. His emphatic entrance made the crowd gasp collectively.

The gigantic screens behind Song lit up with a captivating seascape. Slender palm trees traced the tip of Billionaire Island. Beyond, the expanse of the Andaman Sea blended with the celestial blue. On the pristine sand, a fight ring had been set up. Chatchai turned to the casino's wall-sized windows, which offered an equally-stunning beach view. Comparing the scenery, he ascertained that the video feed was coming from a camera mounted on the palace rooftop. Through the bullet-resistant glass, he could make out the silhouettes of soldiers guarding the ring. It was a few hundred meters further down the shore, a safe distance away.

"Esteemed guests!" Song spoke into a microphone, his English clipped. "I'm very proud to welcome you here for this special occasion. You are about to witness the most spectacular combat in all of martial arts. The Billionaire Bloodbout!"

Isolated claps grew into applause.

Song held up his hand in mock humility.

"It's all about today's contestants! First up, a man unbeaten in all tournaments. Originally from Suriname, the Dutch master of Muay Thai ... Wim Nieuwenhuizen!"

The black Dutchman's intimidating, muscular frame appeared on the left screen in 3D glory, together with his profile. Aged 29, 186 centimeters tall, weighing 97 kilos.

"And fighting against him is the Kyokushin karate champion, the first Russian to complete the *100-man kumite*! Eugene Sokolov!"

The right screen showed an image of a white man in karate uniform. According to the fighter profile, he was slightly older, taller and lighter than his opponent.

Song retrieved a tablet from his Louis Vuitton porte-monnaie to read out the full fighter data, including their illustrious achievements on the martial arts circuit.

"Today, they have the honor of battling at *this* venue."

The middle-screen camera zoomed in on the fight ring. Although standard in shape and size, it was no ordinary boxing ring. Instead of ropes, Chatchai saw strands of barbed wire strung out tightly between the ringposts. Glinting in the sun, shards of broken glass lay strewn all around the canvas.

"Allow me to recap the rules. The Bloodbout is a no-holds-barred match lasting three rounds, ninety seconds each. No referee. Any attempt to escape the ring will be squashed by gunfire. The match continues until the time runs out, or one or both fighters die. The challenge will rise as the fight progresses. At the end of Round One, the barbed wire will be energized to 3,000 volts, forming a lethal electric fence. At the end of Round Two, explosive charges will go off in the danger zone surrounding the ring. Should the tie produce no winner at the end of Round Three, a powerful bomb will detonate in the center of the ring."

Awed murmur spread among the audience.

The extra screen on the left switched to a close-up of Song.

"Gentlemen!" Song exclaimed. "Now is the last chance to place your bets! You can cash out at any time in foreign currency or Bloodcoin. Millions are to be made!"

Indeed, each of Song's guests could easily stake several hundred thousand U.S. dollars at once. The right-hand-side screen displayed the betting odds. The fight seemed evenly balanced. Sokolov to win at 7/4, Nieuwenhuizen a slight favorite at 7/5, and a draw at 23/10. Bonus factors, such as predicting the winning round or defeat by electrocution, promised to multiply the amounts wagered.

From opposite edges of the main screen, soldiers shepherded the two fighters toward the raised platform of the ring.

Song's guttural cry boomed around Billionaire Casino.

"Begin the Bloodbout! *DO OR DIE*!"

10

The foul-smelling, khat-chewing soldiers prodded Sokolov's spine with the muzzles of their AKs, pushing him toward the ring. His body still felt sore after the ordeal inside the cage and he could barely stand on his feet. His jailers and their three comrades secured the beach area around the perimeter of the ring. Trying to flee would spell death. He'd heard the match rules, or lack thereof, over a loudspeaker mounted on a nearby palm tree. He was forced to fight for his life—literally.

Climbing over the barbed wire, he suppressed a wave of anxiety. It was gone as soon as he stepped into the ring. His mind went into mission mode, a familiar zone where nothing else existed apart from the task at hand. He became calm and focused. He'd survived tougher battles. He knew what to do.

Broken glass crunched under his *geta* shoes. Sokolov squinted in the sun, posture relaxed, hands on belt. From the opposite corner, his adversary sized Sokolov up. The Dutch fighter was a mountain of steroid-fueled muscle clothed only in red Muay Thai trunks bearing his name in large white letters, *WIM*, adorned with a dragon design. His hands and feet were wrapped in tape. Wim grimaced, giving Sokolov a vicious stare.

"*Round One!*" blared Song's voice from the loudspeaker, forgoing any pre-match routine.

Instantly, Wim charged across the ring and leaped forward, attacking Sokolov with a flying knee strike. Sokolov raised his arms in a block, absorbing the blow. Both came out of the collision drawing first blood. Wim nicked his foot, landing awkwardly on the shard-strewn floor. Sokolov staggered back from the impact, pressing against the barbed wire and grazing his arm. Mentally, he registered no pain from the cut. Gone, too, was the crushing fatigue, his reflexes as sharp as ever.

The founder of Kyokushin karate, Mas Oyama, had fought

any challenger in no-holds-barred bouts. Likewise, Sokolov was well-versed in different fighting styles and feared no opponent. Wim bounced on his toes like a typical Muay Thai practitioner, his motions fluid. His long limbs offered great reach, probing with jabs and kicks. The threat kept Sokolov pinned back to the edge of the ring. Sokolov flirted dangerously with the barbed wire, his back brushing against it a couple of times. Sensing an opportunity, Wim pounced. He came to close range with a quick jab, low kick combo, which Sokolov parried and countered with his own *mawashi geri* roundhouse. Wim evaded, springing away and immediately slashed at Sokolov's supporting leg. The kick to his tendons jolted Sokolov like a snake bite. He unleashed a series of punches but Wim blocked and dodged them all, dancing around the ring. Sokolov chased him to deliver a killer blow but a thrusting *teep* kick held him back every time. Finally Sokolov came within striking distance and aimed a bare-knuckled lunge punch to the bridge of the nose. He fluffed it by a millisecond and left himself open. Wim ducked, the blow glancing off his head, and punished Sokolov with a spinning backfist which he followed through with a rising axe kick. The backfist jarred his abdomen but Sokolov reacted to Wim's heel crashing down on his face by shooting his arms up, wrists crossed. He trapped the swinging foot between his hands locked in *jyuji uke* and kicked low inside the rear leg which buckled. Wim toppled like a felled tree onto the layer of shattered glass. The Dutchman rolled backward to escape the takedown and sprung to his feet. Glass shards rained off his body as he brushed them off. Specks of blood seeped from the multitude of tiny cuts on his skin.

"*Round Two!*"

During the One-Hundred-Man Kumite, it had taken Sokolov less than two minutes to defeat each opponent. So far, in ninety seconds, he hadn't managed to get anywhere near his agile adversary, who became even more motivated by his sluggish start. Grinning, Wim taunted from the other side of the ring, using obscene gestures. For such a hulk of a man, his speed and endurance were unbelievable. *Performance-enhancing drugs?* Sokolov needed to raise his own level regardless of whatever was giving Wim the edge.

And he could almost hear the 3,000 volts of electricity now buzzing through the barbed wire.

Circling the ring, Wim prepared his onslaught. Sokolov sidestepped, drawing him in. Then Wim lunged with a powerful cross punch and clinched. Grappling around his neck, the Dutchman pummeled Sokolov with a barrage of diagonal knee strikes and elbow chops. Guarding against hits, Sokolov felt like a practice dummy. In rapid *shuto* moves, he first broke free from the clinch with the circular arm motion of *mawashi uke*, rammed the ridge of his knife-hand into Wim's left kidney, and knocked him back with a palm-heel strike to the collarbone. As his opponent reeled, losing balance, Sokolov propelled him across the ring with a sidekick planted into the chest. The sheer force of Sokolov's *yoko geri* sent Wim into a tumbling slide through the razor-sharp glass.

The big Muay Thai fighter grunted in pain as he picked himself up, eyes bulging wildly. He dashed forward in a relentless all-out attack. The strikes descended one after another from every direction, all intended to maim or kill. The Dutchman targeted the vital points of the human body. Landing any of the blows cleanly would crush the throat, neck, solar plexus, temple, kidneys, groin, or ribs for lung damage.

A chaotic melee ensued. Wim's jabs and hooks broke against Sokolov's knife-hand blocks. Sokolov defended from each roundhouse with a shin block and deflected the *teep* kicks by swinging his leg in a hooking motion. He hit back after every parry, but none of his *tsuki* connected with accuracy. The exchange of offensive and defensive actions between the two fighters was frenetic. His opponent's intensity pressured Sokolov to retreat closer to the now-lethal barbed wire.

A fraction of a second gave Sokolov an opening he sought. In his frenzied assault, Wim lingered to pull his leg back from an unsuccessful kick. Sokolov countered. From the blocking *sune uke* position, leg raised, he snapped a front kick into Wim's standing leg which carried his full weight. Sokolov's wooden *geta* heel crushed the kneecap. The Dutch fighter's own 97-kilo mass did the rest.

Roaring in agony, Wim went down like a sack of bricks.

Sokolov twisted his hips, spinning in an unstoppable pirouette of *ushiri mawashi geri*, whipping his leg out, the sole smashing through the opponent's jaw.

Relieved of several teeth, Wim collapsed face-first, kissing the canvas. He would remain sprawled for a while, knocked out. The Dutchman's helpless, prostrate form was completely at Sokolov's mercy. Yet he hadn't the slightest inclination to kill the defeated Muay Thai fighter. He had never intended to murder another man, before or after the Bloodbout. He knew that his opponent wouldn't have shown the same respect and sportsmanship toward him, but the fact couldn't sway Sokolov's principles.

Sokolov doubled over, chest heaving from exhaustion. The extreme physical effort had taken its toll. Seconds passed. Outside the ring, he heard the all-too-familiar sound of an AK charging handle being pulled back to load a 7.62-millimeter round from the magazine.

"Finish him, you idiot!" a Burmese guard shouted to Sokolov in English, training the AK at him. "Or I'll shoot *you!*"

Sokolov wouldn't budge. He wasn't worried about the guard yet, who was holding the AK too casually at his hip. If the soldier wanted to make good on his threat, he would have to come closer and get a better aim. Instead, the guards were backing away, AKs at the ready.

They're keeping a safe distance, he realized a moment too late.

The loudspeaker crackled with Song's voice for the last time. "*Final Round!*"

Abruptly a succession of explosive charges went off around the ring's perimeter. The blast knocked Sokolov down. He fell sideways near the edge of the ring, a whisker away from getting electrocuted by the barbed wire. But as he got back up, he saw that it was only a matter of *how* he would be fried and not *if.* A continuous wall of fire surrounded the ring from all sides. The detonations had set blaze to fuel containers hidden in the sand. The heat was so ferocious that Sokolov felt as if he were stuck inside a furnace. The flames were creeping toward the ringposts. Before long, the conflagration would reach the canvas and roast him alive.

He heard a guttural cry behind him.

Despite the damage he'd suffered, Wim Nieuwenhuizen still came at Sokolov. It was kill or be killed. He was dragging his crippled leg. His lacerated skin was bleeding profusely. By Sokolov's rough estimate, the list of inflicted injuries also included a bruised kidney, fractured collarbone, cracked sternum, broken jaw and smashed nose. Any other man would have required immediate medical attention. Not the Dutch fighter.

He's definitely pumped on dope, Sokolov thought. *But the Bloodbout was never meant to be a fair fight!*

Like a wounded beast, he threw himself at Sokolov in one last desperate attack. He clawed savagely at Sokolov's face with one hand and swung the other, stabbing with a jagged fragment of broken glass. There was no style or strategy involved, just the desire to survive by any means necessary, driven by a primeval instinct.

Sokolov spun out of the way and kicked the Dutchman's upper back with a hooking *kake geri*. Wim lost his footing and the added momentum carried him straight into the fence of barbed wire. Sparks showered. The deadly electric current made quick work of him. The body jerked convulsively. Then the corpse sagged, arms hanging grotesquely, caught between the strands.

One way or another, Wim Nieuwenhuizen had died.

Sokolov gasped for breath. Smoke from the encircling fire filled his nostrils.

The Bloodbout was over. Yet the loudspeaker remained silent. Song never announced the result.

Sokolov remembered Frolov's gloating.

Once you enter the ring, you won't make it out alive. There will be no winner.

Sokolov checked his Breitling, still intact on his left wrist, and counted the seconds.

The bomb beneath the ring was about to detonate.

His eyes searched for an escape route.

If the bomb doesn't kill me, then the flames, electricity or the guards will.

No more time to think and no options to choose.

He dove to the canvas and rolled over the sharp-edged fragments, underneath the taut barbed wire ... and into the raging blaze.

An explosion blew the ring apart.

11

Only seconds after the fight ring exploded, a hovercraft appeared offshore, speeding across the surface of the Andaman Sea at forty knots on a mantle of churning froth. The Red Star on its hull was menacing. It was a *Yuyi*-class LCAC (Landing Craft, Air-Cushioned), operated by the Chinese People's Liberation Army Navy.

The LCAC landed on the beach of Billionaire Island, its huge gas turboprops whining, sand blowing around it. The Chinese hovercraft sprayed seawater from its inflated skirt and 14.5-millimeter rounds from its two twin machine guns. The bullet storm raked the beach, cutting down the patrolling Burmese soldiers, their bodies dropping in red puffs.

Measuring thirty-three meters from bow to stern and sixteen across the beam, the medium-sized LCAC was roughly as large as a gray whale, but unlike a beached sea creature, *this* monster glided along the coastline effortlessly.

No sooner had it hit the shore than Chinese troops disembarked and deployed around the beach. They numbered at least a platoon of two dozen men, all dressed in blue camouflage uniforms and brandishing Type 95 automatic weapons in search of targets. An armored personnel carrier rolled out in support.

Sokolov lay behind the debris of the fight ring. His position helped him remain unnoticed. He had covered himself in sand, smothering the flames which had caught the left pant leg during his jump. His ears were still ringing from the bomb blast.

All five guards keeping watch over the Bloodbout had been shot by the machine guns mounted on the Chinese hovercraft. Miraculously, a volley of rounds buzzed just over his head and snapped a palm tree a few meters behind him into half, as if it were a toothpick.

Sokolov watched the scene unfold in shock. He'd seen a

Russian *Zubr*-class hovercraft, the world's largest with a 150-ton capacity, up close. Although dwarfed by the four-story-tall *Zubr*, the Chinese *Yuyi*-class LCAC was every bit as intimidating in action, as Sokolov had just witnessed first-hand. By their uniforms, Sokolov identified the troops as the Chinese Marine Corps. Probably the Special Operations Force Battalion, which carried out commando missions for the PLA Navy.

They split up into several groups. A four-man protective detail remained at the hovercraft. Eight men entered the APC through the door in the rear. The rest followed the APC on foot. Smoke and the flickering flames obscured Sokolov's view of the LCAC over a hundred meters away. He doubted that any of the Chinese troops could see his figure, much less determine that he had stayed unscathed in the carnage, but he took no chances. He didn't dare move until he'd made sure they were out of sight. In a well-organized formation behind the APC, the Marines proceeded along the beach in the direction of the Billionaire Casino.

The main force advanced toward their objective. So far, the Chinese had shown no interest in searching the demolished Bloodbout venue for survivors, but everything could change at any moment. Billionaire Island kept throwing surprises at him, and he wasn't going to lie around waiting for the next one. His left leg hurting like hell, Sokolov crawled in the sand, avoiding the scattered debris. He picked up an AK from a fallen Burmese.

Then he made a dash for the growth of tropical vegetation.

12

Stacie felt his rancid breath, reeking of alcohol, as Philemon hissed in her ear.

"Just so that you'd know, I was never in favor of killing your aunt. But Father Mark was right, it did bring you out to San Francisco. That old foolish woman signed her own death warrant when she turned the Oltersdorf notebook over to me. Little did she know that by telling me about you, she signed *your* death warrant, too. Tonight you will be sold to the highest bidder among the villa guests. You're useless now. Mark has found the codebook."

She heard a distant thunderclap carried over from the beach. A pre-planned explosion, according to Song's microphone-amplified commentary echoing from within the palatial walls of the Casino.

She shivered, her breathing hurried. Reclining in the deck chair, she scanned the beachfront and saw black plumes of smoke drifting from the location of the fight venue, isolated from view by a row of palm trees. Philemon squeezed her wrist to get her attention.

"It's a shame that your suffering will serve no higher cause. But it won't end anytime soon. You'll remain a prisoner on the island until you die from abuse."

After the extremely intense but short-term euphoria induced by the drugs, her heart raced and she felt as though insects were crawling under her skin, all over her body. The evil priest's words added to her growing psychosis.

"If you feel so sorry," she murmured, "then why don't you kill me now?"

Philemon laughed. "Murder is a sin. I'm here merely to grant absolution from it. Besides, your destiny is out of my hands. It's for Mr. Song to decide. The Bloodbout is losing its shock value, so a new attraction will be required shortly. A fatal gang-rape in front of spectators, perhaps? Now that's something I'd pay money to see."

Another blast sounded, louder than the previous one.

"A lamb for slaughter like that clueless fool Sokolov. He's also paid the ultimate price for not minding his own business. You two share this stupid altruism that has gotten you in the same predicament. Oh, well. Sometimes the blood of Abel needs to be shed for the world to remain in order."

Sickened by him, Stacie averted her eyes from the old man. Now she was hallucinating. She saw a huge vessel approaching the island. Some kind of hovercraft—rather ugly with a pair of massive propellers at the back—was gliding over the water.

Just as it came to a stop at the beach, a strange staccato of sharp cracks sounded.

Gunfire?

It can't be real, she thought. *Why would the island security or the hovercraft shoot at each other?*

It didn't make sense unless ... the island was under attack!

Her doubts evaporated as slugs hit the Casino, pockmarking the nearest wall and shattering windows. And few stray bullets zipped in the air, rippling the surface of the swimming pool in tiny splashes.

Everything was happening so quickly that she just sat there, paralyzed by fear and the sudden realization.

In panic, the Asian call girls ran around screaming. One of them was shot at the edge of the pool and her limp body plunged into the water, diffusing a red hue.

Releasing Stacie's hand, Philemon turned his head sharply toward the beach. In the next instant, his left eye socket exploded in a spray of gore. The bullet exited through the back of his head and he collapsed, going straight to hell. There wasn't a doubt in Stacie's mind about *that*.

Almost catatonic, Stacie stared blankly at his corpse, blood oozing from his skull on the sundeck. Then she willed herself to snap out of her trance. Overcoming her disgust, she bent down to frisk the dead body. She patted the side pockets of his cassock.

The car key! There it was!

Stacie snatched it. She rolled over, getting up from the other side of the lounge chair and ran barefoot across the sundeck as fast as he could.

She knew she had to run *away* from the Casino, instead of trying to hide inside it, to stand any chance of survival. She darted behind the palace, finding the Range Rover Sport parked exactly where Philemon had left it. The car's sensors picked up the signal from the electronic key in her hand, recognized it and unlocked the doors remotely. She climbed in the driver's seat, slammed the door shut, mashed the engine ignition button, yanked the gear lever and floored the accelerator.

The Range Rover lurched forward. But before she managed to break away, a pair of soldiers cut off her escape route. Unlike the island guards, the attackers wore blue uniforms. She turned the wheel sharply. The soldiers fired automatic weapons. The windshield erupted with a web of fractures. Stacie let out a cry and cowered as the car skidded. More bullets peppered the car. Her terror-gripped mind took a moment to register the fact that none of the slugs were penetrating the vehicle. Abruptly, the gunfire ended with two loud pops as the soldiers dropped, taken out by well-placed head shots. Stacie directed her gaze toward the dense tropical growth where the shots had come from. To her astonishment, an AK-toting man dressed in a once-white karate outfit approached the Range Rover. It was the Russian fighter, she realized, and he had just saved her life. He presented a shocking sight, covered in blood and sand, his left trouser scorched. Yet his azure-blue eyes projected equanimity. It made her feel secure. He was her only hope of making it out of there alive.

She reached over to the front-passenger door and pushed it open.

"Are you Eugene Sokolov?" she asked him in Russian.

"*Da*," the tall man grunted as he climbed into the seat next to her. "And what's your name?"

"Anastacia. Stacie."

"You're doing great, Stacie. Keep your cool. But listen, we need to get off the island, fast."

Weakly, she murmured, "There's a seaplane jetty further down the shore."

"Good. I'll drive us there. Fortunately, the car is fully armored. Just get in the back and don't worry about anything. I'll take care of the rest."

13

Inside Billionaire Casino, the gathering of dignitaries turned into a massacre. Smoke and fire filled the palace as 30-millimeter shells hit from the turret-mounted cannon of the Chinese APC. Explosions rocked the Casino, echoed by a cacophony of muted moans and cries from the decimated human mass. Blood slicked the jumble of debris, dead bodies, overturned game tables and torn-off limbs. The bombardment relented as the Chinese Marines stormed the building, gunning down a trio of disoriented Korean officers. A Burmese official hobbling away was dispatched by a quick burst to the forehead. Fanning out, the Marines killed off all survivors methodically. North Korean or Burmese, military or civilian, call girls or croupiers—all were annihilated without mercy.

Song had every wish to avoid a similar fate. Just as the Chinese Marines swarmed the Casino, he pressed a button to activate the on-stage fog machine. Concealed by artificial haze, Song vanished backstage.

He scrambled to safety down a secret passageway, bathed in white fluorescent lighting. It would take him to the beach from the other side of the palace. To save his skin, he had to reach the jetty before the Chinese seized it. A single plane remained after Frolov's departure. There was no alternate escape route.

He clutched the porte-monnaie, which contained the Oltersdorf notebook. He could not allow it to fall into the hands of the Chinese. No doubt it was the reason behind the attack. Billionaire Island had been compromised—but *how*?

The answer awaited him at the end of the passageway. As he was punching a keypad combination to unlock the hidden back door, a gun pressed against the nape of his neck.

"Leaving so soon? I'd like to collect my winnings."

"Chatchai," Song hissed. "How much are the Chinese paying

you?"

"More than you ever offered."

"You've won. Name your price and let me go."

"Oh no, I'm not as stupid as you think," said Chatchai. "It takes some brains to become a triple agent."

Chatchai's brains splattered all over the floor as Song pivoted, wrenched the gun from his grip and blasted his skull.

14

"Stacie, I need you to keep your head down. Lie as low as possible to make sure nobody can see you. Understand?"

"Uh-huh."

She shifted from the rear seat and crouched on the car floor. The position was less than comfortable as the Range Rover sped over beach sand, but she did as he told her without complaint. Slouching low, she pressed her weight against the seat and held tight. Sokolov admired her unfazed response to the life-threatening circumstances. To him, she was an innocent bystander somehow caught up in this mess and he couldn't allow her to get into harm's way. Even though the car was bullet-resistant, no armor was truly bullet-*proof.* Getting Stacie out of a possible line of fire was his first priority. The tinted windows would help her stay out of sight and avoid detection as an easy target. Sokolov's main goal was getting them both safe and sound to the lone seaplane moored at the jetty. He nestled the AK in his lap. Like cars in Thailand, the Range Rover was a left-hand-traffic model, so sitting on the wrong *right* side again felt awkward—but it freed his right hand to shoot.

"How many planes did you see when they brought you here?"

"At least a couple. I can't remember for sure."

"We've got the last one to catch."

"But who's going to pilot it?"

"I am," said Sokolov as he rolled down the window.

A pair of Burmese sentries were on the prowl, alerted by the distant sounds of raging gunfire. Approaching the jetty, Sokolov stuck out the AK through the open window and fired a few short bursts in their direction. Sand geysered at their feet where the bullets hit. Panic-stricken, the hapless guards entertained no thoughts of returning fire and dropped their weapons cowardly.

Holding their hands up, they sprinted away from the advancing Range Rover and vanished behind a cluster of palm trees.

"So much for security," Sokolov said, stopping the car next to the old wooden jetty. Uncertain whether the rickety structure would support the Range Rover's weight, he didn't risk driving onto the boards.

"Stay put until I give you the all-clear sign," he told Stacie.

"Okay."

Sokolov didn't have time to waste. He got out of the car and jogged along the deserted jetty. Loose boards creaked under his feet. Above, the crystal-clear sky was all his. He only had to reach the plane, get Stacie inside and fire up the engines.

The plane sat low in the water thanks to its buoyant hull. Sokolov's trained eye identified the aircraft as a Dornier Seastar. It was a turboprop-powered flying boat. Above the parasol wings, its propellers were mounted facing forward and backward in a push-pull layout. He peered into the Dornier's empty cockpit. With his experience aboard EMERCOM's own Beriev amphibians, Sokolov felt confident about his ability to handle the Dornier.

With just a few more paces separating him from the aircraft, he heard a creaking sound behind him. Caught by surprise, he spun around to see a trapdoor swinging open a couple of meters away. Emerging from the hatch, a man barged forward and shoulder-tackled Sokolov before he could unleash a volley from the AK.

The jetty wasn't as dilapidated as it had seemed. The old wooden boards concealed an engineering feat. Some sort of an underground tunnel ran underneath, providing a safe passage in the event of any contingency. It must have connected the jetty directly with the palace, because the man attacking him was none other than Song. Knocked back by the momentum, Sokolov lost his footing. The AK broke from his grip, sailing over the edge of the jetty, and plopped into the seawater.

Keeping his distance, Song aimed a gun square at Sokolov's forehead. He sized Sokolov up with triumphant glare of his demonic, multicolored eyes. He wouldn't hesitate to pull the trigger; the white tuxedo was already stained with someone else's blood.

"You should have died at the ring, like the fighting dog that you are," said the North Korean. "I'll put you out of your misery. I hate to make your death quick and painless, but unfortunately

I'm under a time constraint. Dealing with the Chinese is the last item on my agenda. Prepare to meet your Christian Maker."

The gold and brown eyes flashed with the cold-blooded resolve which Sokolov had first encountered in Bangkok. Evading the imminent kill shot, Sokolov dove sideways and hit the seawater with a splash.

Enveloped by the coolness of the sea, Sokolov searched for the AK, but to no avail. His vision was too murky and he failed to reach the bottom with his fingers. His water-filled ears picked up the muted sounds of probing gunshots. Hot pain seared his left triceps as a bullet grazed it. Desperate for air, he kicked up and broke the water surface. Now he was a sitting duck. Song zeroed in on him. What he saw in the next instant caught Sokolov unaware.

Engine roaring, the Range Rover raced down the jetty like an enraged bull. Song pivoted a moment too late, unable to escape the bone-shattering collision. The front bumper and grill of the Range Rover smashed into Song's knees, flinging him like a dummy, feet flipping skyward. His head banged against the windshield. The body bounced off the car's hood and crashed down into the path of the Range Rover's wheels. The armored SUV ran him over with its crushing two-ton weight and left the limp body behind.

Braking, the Range Rover ran out of space and soared off the end of the jetty into the sea. The SUV started sinking fast. With powerful strokes, Sokolov swam toward it. By the time he got near, the car had already gone under. Sucking in a lungful of air, he submerged.

The car had almost filled with water. It was both good news and bad. The bullet-resistant window was unbreakable, and the door would not open until the pressure difference stabilized at least partially as the water flowed in. On the other hand, Sokolov could ill afford to lose precious seconds. Stacie was unconscious. A cut was bleeding above her eyebrow, received during the impact. As the Range Rover descended to the bottom, filling with water, Sokolov's chances of rescuing her diminished rapidly. He pulled the door with all his might until it yielded, and pulled Stacie through the opening. Holding her tightly, he pushed off the car and followed a trail of air bubbles as he dragged her to the surface.

Once they broke clear, he placed his forearms under her armpits, keeping her head securely above the water as he kicked his feet for steady propulsion.

Stacie gagged. Her eyelashes fluttered. Her wet hair was a mess, the make-up had washed off, but to him she looked more gorgeous than ever. Above all, she was alive. She turned her head, realizing that she was in his arms, heading for safety.

"You told me to wait in the car," she said. "I did."

"Very funny."

"You took your time. I was beginning to harbor doubts."

"Thanks for saving my life, but please don't attempt such stunts ever again. You almost drowned, you know."

"I just wanted to try out the swimsuit."

He towed her to the jetty and helped her out of the water.

The Dornier Seastar awaited.

"Come on, let's get out of here," he said as he hoisted himself onto the wooden boards, the soaked *gi* clinging to his muscular frame.

"Hold on a second," Stacie replied.

Instead of heading to the flying boat, she approached the broken body of Song. The North Korean lay motionless on the wooden boards, blood streaking down his face from the gash on his head.

She picked up the item which he had dropped. It was a men's designer handbag. A Louis Vuitton, judging by the distinct monogram pattern. She unzipped the porte-monnaie and browsed its contents until she found a brown leather-bound notebook.

PART III

1

Never in her five years of working as a concierge had Umaporn seen anything like it. And truth be told, she had seen quite a lot at the Front Desk of the Inthurat Resort and Spa, Phuket. It was the island's most luxurious hotel, and one of the very few situated directly on Patong Beach. Enjoying the prime location of the private 200-meter beachfront strip, Umaporn had the perfect view of the Andaman Sea through the lobby's windows.

At first, it was the sound she had heard. A low whining noise, growing louder. Then she saw it, a white shape in the sky, realizing that the whine belonged to the aircraft's engines. The plane was flying low over the waves, the shape becoming more distinct as it neared rapidly. Then its hull skimmed the water and touched down. Its weird top-mounted propeller spinning, the flying boat cleaved through the sea waves toward the beach right in front of the Inthurat Resort and Spa.

The arrival of the amphibian turned heads and evoked gleeful exclamations among those hotel guests who were witnessing it. A German pensioner sipping ice tea in the lobby stared over the top of his spectacles in sheer amazement. At the pool, an excited American couple cheered and snapped photos. The annoying, sunscreen-smeared French children were running around the beach, animatedly pointing and shouting to their parents. Umaporn herself stood fascinated but completely at a loss as to how she should deal with the situation.

As its landing gear wheels touched the sand, the sleek aircraft halted not a hundred meters away from the reception desk. The engines shut down and the plane's cockpit door opened. Two people debarked, a man and a woman. Leisurely, they strolled past the gawking hotel guests, as if it were the most ordinary day in their lives, a mundane commute. The woman was a leggy blonde, clad in a compelling swimsuit. Her stunning appearance prompted an even livelier reaction than the manner of her arrival.

The tall, powerfully-built man who accompanied her was obviously the plane's pilot, although he wasn't dressed to look the part. He wore pants rolled up to knee length together with ridiculous wooden sandals. His sculpted torso was bare from the waist up, his left upper arm bandaged. As he and his female companion entered the hotel, Umaporn also noticed an expensive Swiss watch on his wrist and a Louis Vuitton bag in his hand. Then Umaporn's mind registered the fact that they were heading toward the reception desk. She got a hold of herself and flashed her best smile.

"*Sawasdee*. May I help you, sir?"

Nonchalantly, he said, "We'd like to have your best suite. Do you accept Bloodcoin?"

2

The confused look on the concierge's face told Sokolov that cryptocurrency still had a long way to go until it became a valid payment method at the Inthurat Resort and Spa. The Thai girl standing behind the reception desk certainly didn't appreciate Sokolov's humor. He let the matter drop and instead retrieved a wad of Baht bills from the porte-monnaie. He placed a large portion of the cash atop the desk, paying far in excess of the quoted fee.

"Keep the change."

His passport, soggy and deformed after his underwater escapade, was made acceptable by the generous tip.

The immaculately-garbed receptionist shot a scornful glance at Stacie.

"We appreciate your discretion, Umaporn," said Sokolov, noting the name on her badge. He peeled off a few more Baht notes which she slipped from the desk instantly. No further questions were raised.

Beaming, Umaporn clasped her hands together and bowed.

"*Khob khun ka.* Enjoy your stay."

The Royal Suite lived up to its name. It measured a whopping 300 square meters and featured three separate bedrooms and bathrooms, an enormous lounge, and a dining room with a hand-carved table which seated eight. The furnishings carried a Thai-inspired theme, from hardwood flooring and plush fabrics to beautifully crafted sculptures and paintings.

The suite offered them a balance of privacy and security. On the one hand, the space was so huge that Sokolov and Stacie avoided the awkwardness of being virtual strangers who had to share living quarters. On the other, staying together meant that Sokolov didn't have to worry about Stacie's safety. It also allowed them to pose as a couple, diverting undue attention. The exclusive status granted seclusion from other guests. Apart from a picturesque vista of Patong Beach, the suite's private patio also provided an avenue of escape in case of emergency. Overall, Sokolov was content with the arrangement. He got Umaporn to fetch a change of clothes for himself and Stacie at the hotel's luxury store and ordered room service from an award-winning restaurant.

While Stacie occupied the in-suite spa, Sokolov retreated to his own bathroom and took stock of the damage to his body. Back aboard the seaplane, the first aid kit had come in handy, enabling him to treat the worst injuries quickly. Now he saw that he'd gotten off easy. His left leg hurt, but the burns on his calf were superficial. The discomfort was negligible compared to the nearly-suffered cremation. The gunshot wound proved to be no more than a scratch, the slug's lethal velocity negated by the water. He expected the wounds to heal quickly. He showered, applied a new dressing to his arm, and donned a navy polo, matching slacks and comfortable loafers.

Joining him for lunch, Stacie entered the dining room, attired in all white: a long-sleeved silk shirt, tight shorts and lace-up sandals. With her golden hair, she looked angelic. A defenseless guardian angel.

She appeared refreshed both physically and mentally but Sokolov could see a plaintive shadow behind those sparkling amethyst eyes.

"It feels great to be celebrating life again," she said, sipping a glass of pineapple juice.

Sokolov toasted his own tropical drink in agreement.

"So, here we are," he said. "We might as well figure out why."

He told her his part of the story, beginning with his EMER-COM background. She recounted the details of her trip to San Francisco and everything that had happened since.

"They murdered my aunt," Stacie concluded. "She had confided in them as priests. She had trusted them to guard her secret. Instead, they killed her, whoever they really are. And they used her trust to try and kill me. The man calling himself Father Mark has stolen my pendant. I'll go to Hong Kong and get it back."

"You can't. They'll try to kill you again, and they might succeed this time. For your own sake, you should return to Australia."

"Do you think they won't reach me back home? They know where I live. And even if I went back to Sydney, my life would never be the same. They believe I'm a lamb for slaughter but I'll show them how wrong they are. When I first learned of the Oltersdorf legacy, I wanted to serve a worthy cause. Right now, for me there is no cause worthier than getting even. I'll make Father Mark pay, whether you like the idea or not."

He attempted to talk her out of it but she stood her ground with steely determination. There was no dissuading her from going to Hong Kong.

"Let's just get out of here and then we can walk our separate ways," she said.

"I'm afraid our ways are no longer separate, Stacie. There's no telling where your involvement begins or mine ends, with all those North Korean spies and Russian priests. But you're right, we can't do anything as long as we're stranded in Phuket."

After they had finished the signature avocado-and-seafood salad by a celebrity chef, Sokolov examined the Louis Vuitton handbag. The spoils included the remainder of the cash, a gaming token from Billionaire Casino and a tablet which looked very similar to the one formerly owned by Kinkladze. He powered it on. While the tablet booted, Sokolov fiddled the casino token in his hand. All of a sudden, the tablet and the token interacted wirelessly. Sokolov realized that it wasn't just a gaming chip he was holding between his fingers, but a near-field-communication device. An electronic wallet. Reading the NFC tag embedded in the token, the tablet immediately opened the account status. It showed a balance of 492,500 Bloodcoin. Sokolov hadn't the faintest idea about the exchange rates between various cryptocurrencies and real money, but he assumed that Song had carried a substantial amount to cover his needs.

Sokolov closed the wallet app and fired up the browser. The familiar message greeted him.

`Welcome to the Dark Web`

He pushed the red *Enter* button and typed in the passcode, which he had committed to memory. Bringing up the search bar, he checked the flight schedule at Phuket International Airport. The nationwide protests had affected domestic flights in and out of Phuket, but the international terminal was operating as usual. In the upcoming hours, only two destinations were listed under Departures: Singapore and Hong Kong. Boarding had already commenced for the Singapore Airlines flight. The next one later that day had been fully booked, hardly surprising with Changi acting as a major hub for connecting flights all around the Asia-Pacific.

Planes traveling to Hong Kong departed five times a day with plenty of options available.

Hong Kong it was, then.

"Destiny," said Stacie. "The Creator is guiding our fate. Accept it."

He did.

Choosing the destination was the first step. They still lacked any travel documents.

Sokolov launched the Dark Web browser and navigated through the categories of the Hidden Wiki.

`Fake ID.`

He tapped on the link.

A chat window opened. The anonymous contact was online and marked as a favorite. Song must have procured forged documents regularly. *Perhaps this is how he obtained that Russian passport for Alex Grib*, thought Sokolov. With the chat history cleared, there was no way of making sure. Sokolov had to trust his gut instinct.

He sent a message in English, hoping that he didn't need to employ some sort of code.

Need 2 passports ASAP.

With growing apprehension, he waited for a reply. Finally, it came in a single word.

Details

He typed:

M, the same Russian. F, a young blonde.

Default delivery address?

No. Inthurat Resort, Phuket.

OK. 1 hour.

A notification bubble popped up, prompting him to pay the required sum. He hit the CONFIRM TRANSFER button. Instantly, the Bloodcoin balance reduced by 1,200.

The contact went offline.

In one hour, Sokolov would learn whether he'd placed the winning bet. He was wagering with much more than Bloodcoin.

3

Sokolov found no way around the password protection of the email interface. If he wanted to recover Song's email conversations, he'd have to leave it for later and let Pavel Netto work his magic. The incognito VoIP client, however, required no login. He dialed a private number.

"Who the hell is this?" Klimov's gruff voice came through the tablet's speaker, sounding crystal clear over the high-quality data connection.

"It's Sokolov."

"Thank God you're alive!" said his boss with a sigh of relief.

"What about Zubov and Mischenko?" asked Sokolov, concerned for the well-being of his crew.

"They're fine. They've just returned from Don Muang and told me that you bargained for their release. I gave them the hairdryer treatment for leaving you behind."

"You shouldn't have. You know they'd never let me down. There was nothing else they could do at that point."

"We sure can do something now that you've showed up. Where the hell are you?"

"I'm working on getting out of Thailand. I need the boys to pick me up in Hong Kong."

"No sweat. They'll be more than happy to fly in right away."

"And I'll be more than happy to see them. This mission has been one hell of a pain in the neck, Minister."

"Tell me about it, Gene. Our so-called friends opposite the Bolshoi have gone very quiet on the whole thing." The EMERCOM Headquarters neighbored the Bolshoi Theater from one side and the old KGB building from the other. "I imagine that something went very wrong, blowing right back into their faces."

"Like you wouldn't believe," Sokolov confirmed.

"Get to my office for a full debriefing, first thing. Just try to get back home in one piece, Gene," said Klimov.

"Trust me, I'm trying my damnedest."

Next, Sokolov rang up Constantine on his cell phone.

"Hey, brother."

"Gene! Are you all right?"

"More or less. You?"

"Much better than I was yesterday, thanks to your call. What have you been up to? You do have something on your mind, don't you?"

He chuckled. "You know me better than anyone. I'm in a spot of bother with a historical mystery."

"History? Do tell."

"Does the name Oltersdorf sound familiar?"

"Hmmm. It does seem to ring a bell. I think it's the name of a Russian general during the First World War. Yes, Baron Peter Oltersdorf. What about him?"

"I need to find the connection between the Russian Church and North Korean spies. Somehow, it revolves around Oltersdorf."

"Quite a mystery, indeed. The Russian Church? Do you mean the Moscow Patriarchate?"

"I believe so."

"I know just the right man who can help us," said Constantine. "Where are you and when are you coming back?"

"I'm in Phuket right now."

"So while I'm sulking in this miserable weather, my kid brother goes on vacation in Thailand," Constantine joked.

Eugene grinned. The brothers had gone through thick and thin together since early childhood, always looking after each other.

"Yeah, and I'm staying with a jaw-dropping beauty in my room, as well. She's the baron's descendant." Then he added seriously, "I wish it were a holiday trip, but in fact it's been quite the opposite. And it's not over yet. Hopefully, I'll be en route to Moscow in a few hours. We can meet tomorrow or the day after."

"Great, I'll dig up something in time for your return. My curiosity is certainly piqued."

"Thanks. See you soon."

Sokolov consulted the dial of his Breitling. The designated hour was fast approaching. He came over to the lobby for early recon. Picking a suitable spot, he sat at a table which gave him a good view of the main entrance and the Front Desk. He pondered how to deal with the delivery person, if indeed one would show up on such short notice. With limited experience of underhand dealings involving ID purchase, he didn't know what to expect. He couldn't discount the possibility of a set-up run by local cops. In that case, his position enabled him to rush back to the suite, grab Stacie and flee via the patio exit.

He ordered a soda, and no sooner had the waiter brought the beverage than Sokolov heard the sputtering of an engine in the street. He peered outside through the nearest window and saw a *tuk-tuk*—the local variety of a motorized rickshaw—pull over at the hotel's entrance.

A teen got out from the back of the shabby three-wheeled vehicle. The Thai kid, inconspicuous in his checkered shirt, baggy pants and baseball cap, walked through the front door, toting a rucksack. He stopped at the reception desk, opened the flap of his rucksack and extracted a manila envelope from within its depths. He exchanged a few phrases in Thai with Umaporn as he handed her the envelope. Then the young courier bowed and marched back to the waiting *tuk-tuk*, which zoomed away, coughing black exhaust as soon as he clambered inside.

Sokolov left his drink untouched and crossed the lobby. Umaporn surrendered the envelope, given to her just seconds ago by the errand boy. Thanking her, he collected it and quickly withdrew from the lobby.

He noted the handwritten marking, scrawled on the envelope in crude letters:

For S.

Ironically, it must have implied Song, but inside he hoped to find something for Stacie and himself.

As soon as he returned to the Royal Suite, he ripped the envelope open. To his satisfaction, he discovered two passports within it. He studied both carefully with mixed impressions. The IDs hadn't been forged, but rather stolen.

One passport was British, in the name of Calum McKinley. Staring from the mugshot, Mr. McKinley hardly shared any likeness with Eugene Sokolov. If anything, the physiognomy appeared vaguely similar to the features of Alex Grib. Quite unfortunately, McKinley had a bald patch on the top of his head. Sokolov would have to make do. He examined the other passport, which gave him more reason to cheer.

Emphatically, he presented it to Stacie.

"Stacie Rose, I hereby pronounce you Federica Buonamano."

"You *what*?"

"From now on, you're a citizen of the Italian Republic, at least for the time being."

With incredulity crossing her face, she plucked the little burgundy-covered booklet from his grasp and inspected it suspiciously. Her eyebrows arched.

"Are you kidding? This woman looks nothing like me!"

"You bear a passing resemblance, and believe me, it's more than enough."

She giggled. "You're crazy."

"That's beside the point. Lots of people look different from their own photos. Especially those women who are always changing their hairstyles, applying layers of make-up, wearing contact lenses, and undergoing cosmetic procedures that can make them unrecognizable over the years. The real Federica Buonamano has your hair color and face shape, which is a big plus. Border officials are too overworked to analyze each passport picture for discrepancies."

Sokolov recounted the search-and-rescue effort surrounding the disappearance of Malaysian Airlines Flight MH370. The resulting investigation had exposed Phuket as the world's biggest marketplace for fake IDs. Two Iranians had boarded the missing plane using EU passports stolen from tourists visiting Thailand.

"Some foreigners even sell their passports to locals for a quick buck," Sokolov explained. "When you show your passport to immigration officers, they are mainly concerned whether it has all the required entry or exit stamps and a valid visa. Sometimes they run the passport number through an Interpol database, but the flood of international passengers is so huge that they only do it if they have strong misgivings. This passport is genuine. That's the most important thing. Nobody will have reason to question your integrity as the legitimate holder. Don't worry, we can work on your Federica Buonamano look. You *are* a photo model, anyway."

Stacie pouted. "All right, I believe you, Eugene Sokolov. Or what should I call you now?"

Sokolov grinned. "Mr. McKinley."

"Well then, Mr. McKinley. I've already been fooled once trying to reach Hong Kong. How could I trust anyone if it happened again? Although I look into your eyes and see that you're an honest man."

"Oh, there'll be plenty of fooling. But this time, you'll be the one doing it."

4

Located twenty kilometers north of Patong Beach in a rural area of Phuket, surrounded by 42 acres of land, stood the Holy Trinity Church. The newly built cathedral measured 25 meters in height, topped by a six-meter-tall golden cupola, making it the largest church of the Moscow Patriarchate in Thailand.

Flavian, né Georgi Kirilenko, had it all to himself. He regarded it as his personal ranch. He'd never had it so good. But what the hell, he deserved it. Damned right he did. All those years serving the SVR in different hellholes around the globe had earned him the payoff. He led a comfortable lifestyle in one of the world's most coveted travel destinations and got paid for it. Who needed heaven in the *afterlife* when he'd found paradise in the *present* life? He relished the island's tropical coziness by day and satiated his bisexual tastes on Bangla Road by night. Indeed, Colonel Georgi Kirilenko, or Hierodeacon Flavian as he was now known, was enjoying his best years.

He was sitting on a bench, watching as a pair of his horses grazed on a grassy field, when his cell phone buzzed. He dug the mobile from the pocket of his gray cassock. It was Javad Habibi, the Iranian.

Flavian stroked his trimmed beard pensively. Javad Habibi was the key man in a human-trafficking syndicate operating in Phuket. The onus was greater than ever on the 45-year-old Iranian. Recently, the DSI had busted the gang's Pattaya branch, arresting Habibi's associates and confiscating over a thousand stolen passports. Habibi had been extra cautious ever since. Flavian was under direct orders from the Patriarchate to assist Habibi in any way possible, so he answered the phone, albeit reluctantly.

"Yes?"

"I got word from your Korean guy," said Habibi in Persianaccented English, drawing out the syllables.

"I see." The man in question was Song, Flavian understood.

"Maybe it's no big deal, but ... He suddenly ordered two items. I find it strange because he didn't like to have it delivered to your place as usual."

"Oh?"

"Yes, he told me to send it to a hotel instead of picking it up from you. It's him, of course, de message came from his device. I did like he said, but... I fink I must let you know."

"Yes, thank you. You said two items?"

"For man and for woman. I give you de numbers."

"Okay."

Habibi broke the connection.

Flavian fired up his brain cells. It was most unusual for Song to be acting that way. The Holy Trinity Church had always served as a dead drop site in such matters. Perhaps Flavian, like Habibi, was giving it too much thought. Better safe than sorry.

He forwarded the passport numbers to his paid contact at the airport, a fifteen-minute drive from the church. Minutes later, the airline staff member informed him that the passports had just been used to purchase two business-class tickets to Hong Kong.

Whatever was going on, Father Flavian decided to alert Father Mark in Hong Kong. What else were friends for? Their friendship ran a long way back to the days of the KGB spy school in Minsk.

5

Ninety kilometers per hour. The needle of the speedometer crept past the mark as Constantine pressed the accelerator. One hundred. He pushed the Audi Q5 further.

Constantine hurried to beat the early evening rush heading out of Moscow. Failing to do that, he could get stuck for several hours as the highway came to a standstill. What he kept telling his students held true for Moscow's insane traffic—it, too, was a problem rooted in the communist past: a combination of poor urban planning, lack of infrastructure, terrible road maintenance, and barbaric driving manners. Other motorists were darting between lanes, cutting in front of the Audi as they avoided potholes.

Constantine was heading north-east, seventy kilometers away from the capital, to the town of Sergiev Posad, home of the Trinity St. Sergius Lavra. Darkness was already descending, and it was pitch black by the time he reached the town's dimly lit streets, which were still marred by socialist architecture and Bolshevik names.

The Trinity Lavra, a monastery founded in the early fourteenth century by St. Sergius, the patron saint of Russia, had flourished as the country's main nexus of culture and religion for almost 600 years. Today, although it remained active, it had become little more than a landmark of a vanished civilization, and a tourist attraction. Constantine hoped to encounter few tourists or pilgrims at such a late hour. He parked the Audi off the Red Army Prospekt, blasphemously named in honor of the monastery's looters, and walked to the ancient white walls of the religious complex, entering through the frescoed Holy Gates.

He found his way around the alleys connecting a plethora of churches and chapels. Crossing the main plaza of the Monastic Square, he strolled past the Theological Academy and the

Monastery proper toward the Trinity Cathedral. It was the Lavra's most dominant church, as well as the oldest, built in 1422. The sanctum sanctorum.

A shadowy figure exited the Trinity Cathedral. A priest, wearing a gold-colored cope over his cassock, was leaving after the night service.

It must be him, Constantine thought.

"Father Mikhail!" he called.

The black-bearded, black-cassocked priest froze, turning his head.

"Father Mikhail, may I have a word with you?"

"I'm listening."

Constantine approached the middle-aged priest in front of the Cathedral's stone wall, both men silhouetted by the outdoor illumination. The priest eyed him intently.

"You know who I am," said Constantine. "And you also know why I'm here."

"I don't follow you. Now if you'll excuse me—"

"Ilia. The person I must meet. Metropolitan Ilia. Where is he?"

"I'm sorry but Metropolitan Ilia is dead. He entrusted his pure soul to God a few months ago."

"We both know full well that he's alive. All these months he's been hiding somewhere inside the Lavra. If he's no longer staying here, then I'd like you to tell me where I may find him. You can drop the act, Father."

"Young man, I shall call the police unless you leave at once!"

Constantine was growing frustrated but he understood why the priest felt so protective of Ilia. Constantine's actions had placed Ilia in mortal danger, both of them falling for an elaborate ruse conducted by the then-FSB Director Saveliy Frolov.

"It's all right," said a voice behind Constantine. "Don't worry, Mikhail. This young man is my disciple. He's a friend. I'm so glad to see you, Constantine. I had a vision today. An archangel told me that you would arrive here to visit me."

Constantine turned around to face his former mentor. Wrinkled, white-bearded, his frail body supported by a cane, Ilia appeared much older than Constantine remembered him. But his eyes were as lucid as ever. A knot tightened in Constantine's chest. At one point, Ilia had become something of a father figure to him. He'd seen his real father die live on television as a kid. And during their last meeting, he'd seen Father Ilia bleed to death, shot before his very eyes. Or so Constantine had believed. He suppressed the painful memories, grateful that the old priest was alive.

"Come, my child, let's go for a walk."

Cane tapping against the stone walkway, Ilia ambled toward the nearest bench.

"I remember the first time when you came to seek guidance. You had so much youthful energy. You wanted to right the wrongs, to cure the ailments that our country has been suffering for a century."

"I was too naïve, Holy Father."

He helped Ilia ease his body to the bench and sat next to the old man. In the semi-darkness, he listened to Ilia's soft voice.

"You shared my passion, Constantine. You dreamt of a tribunal against communism. Their overdue Nuremberg Trials which they had escaped. A taste of justice at The Hague. Tell me, have you given up the fight?"

"A Russian renaissance breaking out of Soviet slavery? It was but an illusion. I know I'm fighting a lost cause. Even so, I'm not ready to throw in the towel just yet. Especially now. This time, it's my brother who could find himself in great peril."

"Eugene? I remember him."

Constantine nodded. "Gene has stumbled upon something even I can't understand. It is because of my ignorance and inexperience that I request your help once more."

"If there's any way I can help you, I will. What is your question?"

"How could the Moscow Patriarchate get mixed up with North Korean communists?"

Ilia sighed. "Sometimes it takes a lifetime to see the truth. I was trapped in a web of deceit for too long, I believed I was acting for the greater good. I let my illusions take over me, and no one is guiltier than me for imposing my own illusions upon you. Half-truths can be even more dangerous than lies. It ends here. A mortician can embalm a rotting corpse only so much until it finally decomposes."

Constantine was only beginning to grasp the implications of what Ilia was saying, but the old priest's words frightened him.

"When communism formally fell in Russia, for a brief moment the KGB archives erupted like a volcano," said Ilia.

"They sealed the lid pretty quickly," Constantine replied.

"Some damaging evidence flowed out nonetheless. Remember what I told you about the ties between the KGB and the clergy?"

"You said that the church was rife with KGB infiltrators. A significant number of clerics were KGB agents. You wanted to weed them out."

"Yes, that is exactly what I said. And it's a bitter pill to swallow. Forgive me, Constantine."

With mounting uneasiness, he asked, "Why are you asking forgiveness, Father?"

"I wasn't honest with you, my child. I *lied* to you."

Constantine stared in disbelief. "How?"

"I twisted the facts to suit my own needs. It wasn't a large portion of church clergy who were KGB agents. *All* of them worked for the KGB."

"No ... " Constantine breathed.

"I know that because I did, too. I was a KGB agent myself."

6

The shocking words rocked Constantine to the core, but it was just the beginning.

I'm not a priest, he'd once told another man in France.

Now he was.

In the cold of the night, he listened to the confession of his former mentor. And indeed, Constantine was the only one who could abolish his sins.

As if mindful of unseen eavesdroppers, Ilia spoke in a low voice.

"The Moscow Patriarchate never existed until 1943. Whichever way you look at it, *de jure* and *de facto*, it is a creation of Joseph Stalin. He himself coined the term. Christianized in 988, Russia joined the Byzantine Church. Later, in 1453 the Russian Church declared autocephaly, becoming the Eastern Orthodox Russian Church. And so it lasted until the twentieth century. Then came the dirty, Germany-sponsored coup d'état, touted as the *Revolution*. Some wrongly assume that the Bolshevik regime was atheist. In fact, it was theomachist. Not just denying God's existence, but *fighting* Him. And you don't battle against something you don't believe in. The so-called civil war waged by the Bolsheviks was a religious war, first and foremost. Members of a bizarre cult set out to destroy anyone who didn't convert to their devilish ways. The murder of Czar Nicholas II, the Lord's anointed sovereign, together with the Royal Family, was purely ritual, a sacrifice to Satan. The Red Terror forced millions to bow down in submission and worship the blood-red pentagram while many more millions endured inhuman suffering. The Bolsheviks burned icons and pillaged churches, ransacked monasteries and desecrated graveyards. They raped nuns to death, disemboweled priests and hanged them by their intestines, disfigured bodies, boiled and buried people alive, tore babies to pieces before the eyes of their mothers, shot, slashed, impaled and dismembered those who would not renounce the Christian faith. Even thinking about these horrors may cause the sanest of men to lose their minds. But perpetrating such heinous acts? Or turning a blind eye like the world did? Truly, the end of days is nigh. May the Lord bless the souls of Russia's martyrs."

Ilia crossed himself, gazing at the dark sky for a few moments.

"As a result," he continued, "by the end of the new wave of terror in 1937, all of the Russian clergy had been killed or imprisoned, the churches defiled or reduced to rubble. Effectively, the Orthodox Russian Church ceased to exist, annihilated."

"But what happened in 1943?" asked Constantine.

"The war changed everything. Stalin and his cronies faced the gravest danger they had ever encountered. Millions of Russian men surrendered to the Germans, unwilling to shed their blood for the sake of Stalin's hide."

Constantine remembered the sobering words once spoken by Eugene:

Stalin's peace was worse than Hitler's war.

"He had to throw them a bone," Constantine surmised. "Slogans of world communism and proletarian paradise didn't cut it anymore after a taste of that so-called paradise. So the Bolshevik deceivers made a U-turn toward patriotism and God."

"There's something else you need to consider. The Nazis did a lot of evil when they came to Russia, but for propaganda reasons, they did not oppress Christianity. All across occupied Russia, a captive nation rediscovered faith. Despite the wartime hardships, people toiled to reopen their churches and organize parishes. The movement was popular, uplifting—and uncontrolled. If left unchecked, it could turn into a full-fledged second baptism of Russia. After twenty-five years of trying to eradicate Christianity and break the will of the people, Stalin could not allow it. He had to hold an iron-fisted grip on this and all other attempts at spiritual recovery. Thus, on September 3rd, 1943, he established an entity called the *Russian Orthodox* Church of the Moscow Patriarchate. This new organization was a department of the NKVD, and later the KGB. As a wily conman, Stalin reworded the name of the *Orthodox Russian* Church which he had destroyed, to trick the common man into believing that it was the very same Russian Church which had existed for centuries."

"And the Moscow Patriarchate? Was there any special meaning the title was supposed to carry?"

"Stalin placed a puppet Patriarch of Moscow as the head of his fake church, sending a clear message: *You have your parishes, but no religious leader. Here is your Patriarch, and he's in Moscow. He acknowledges my rule, and so will you.*"

"Instead of serving Christ, the Patriarch worshipped Stalin."

"Like everyone else in Stalin's church, he was a Red. From the very beginning, the Moscow Patriarchate was conceived as an arm of the secret police. Its purpose was two-fold. Firstly, to take control over the surviving vestiges of religious life. Aiding SMERSH and NKVD units who combed the recaptured Soviet territory, the Patriarchate sought out genuine priests and believers. Unawareness of the Patriarchate's true nature condemned many to the gulags. Secondly—and this is perhaps even more treacherous—the guise of the Russian Church covered up the continued persecution of Christians in the Soviet Union for decades to come, with the oppressors themselves masquerading behind it. And with millions of true Christians already slaughtered, nobody could oppose the Red Church. Stalin's iron grip firmly tightened on Russia's throat, this time for good, if not forever."

Silence descended. Constantine's mind protested. A part of him refused to accept the finality of Ilia's indictment.

"No, I can't believe that all is lost," he murmured. "The real Russian Church can't be dead! Someone had to fight the Red Church. Millions of Russian refugees fled from the Bolsheviks, scattering around the world. The last of the White Movement. The Russia *outside* Russia. And among them were the priests who joined their flock in exile. The Russian Orthodox Church Outside Russia."

"Quite right. The Orthodox Church Abroad carried the torch of Russian religious tradition. It was the spiritual backbone of every expatriate community. But, like you said, the Russo-Soviet Civil War had no end date. The Bolsheviks never ceased their efforts to destroy those who had escaped their clutches. For decades, the Reds conducted meticulous work to corrupt the Church Abroad. Bolshevik agents flooded the Russian communities across Europe and America, using deception, propaganda, bribery and assassinations to undermine the true Church from within. And they succeeded. Man is weak, more so when he is separated from his roots. Some fell for the communist lies about the evolution of the Kremlin regime. Others suffered so many hardships in the West that they yearned for a return their homeland. The old, unbreakable generation gradually passed away, replaced by youngsters who had never known Russia or witnessed the horrors of Soviet life for themselves. The power of the Church faded; the resolve to fight for Russia's liberation waned as time passed. Ultimately, the Church could no longer pose any threat to the Reds. A shadow of its former self, and of Russia's past glory. The Church Abroad reached its nadir in 2007. After years of KGB subversion, the top hierarchy signed an act of unconditional surrender at a ceremony in Moscow. What they called a homecoming was a traitorous capitulation before the Moscow Patriarchate and the devilish forces behind it."

"But why did Moscow force the takeover of the Church Abroad? The Patriarchate could have waited until its sworn enemy decayed completely and perished into oblivion once and for all. What was the point of acting out this phony reunion?"

"Expansion. The merger gave the Moscow Patriarchate full control over four hundred parishes around the world, half of them in the United States alone. The Kremlin could only dream of gaining such a foothold on U.S. soil. Immediately, Moscow sent hundreds of spies in the guise of priests all across America. Imagine an espionage network spanning from New York, New Jersey and Pennsylvania to Florida, Texas and California, operating under a well-established church cover. In Washington, DC, the Orthodox Cathedral of St. John the Baptist is located three miles away from the White House. And it's not just the FSB or the SVR accessing these intelligence assets. The Kremlin has made them available to North Korea. Moscow and Pyongyang have set up a secret link via the Patriarchate."

The puzzle pieces were falling into place, but Peter Oltersdorf still didn't fit in.

"Seizing control of the churches, the Moscow Patriarchate must have also captured the vast archives of the White Movement," Constantine surmised. "A wealth of documents, memoirs, letters and testimonies. Do you know any information about Peter Oltersdorf?"

"Oltersdorf? Allegedly, the KGB spent decades hunting for his papers. But they were off-limits until the Church Abroad succumbed to the Patriarchate. Since then, Moscow has scoured the newly acquired church records in every parish all the way to Canada, trying to track his descendants to no avail. I have no idea about the contents of the Oltersdorf papers, so I'm afraid I can't help you—but there's someone who can. His name is Yakov Orlovsky. His father converted me to true Orthodoxy."

"What do you mean?"

"You see, no matter which diabolic doctrines the Bolsheviks effected, they failed to exterminate Christianity *inside* Russia. From the outset of the hellish communist rule, a group of true Christian believers went underground. Even during the most gruesome years, they managed to carry out their activities in secret. The world's most oppressive regime could not squash the Catacomb Church, as it became known. This hidden community fought back."

"How?" asked Constantine.

"Espionage. Fighting fire with fire. Some members of the Catacomb Church infiltrated the Patriarchate. The plan was doomed from the beginning, but one of their ideas was to reform the Red Church from inside. When I was still a young priest, a deacon approached me, carefully probing my attitude toward the Communist Party. Deacon Alexei, he introduced himself. According to the rules, I should have reported our conversation to the KGB immediately. If I didn't, and it proved to be a KGB decoy to test me, I would have faced twenty-five years in the gulags. But in the end, I didn't—couldn't force myself to do it. And by the Lord's grace, nothing happened. Nobody broke into my room in the middle of the night to arrest me. It was then that I really started believing in God."

"Odd to hear that you found religion only after years of priesthood."

"Growing up, I was a peasant boy, nothing but cannon fodder in the eyes of Red commissars. Nonetheless, after I was wounded on the Eastern Front, I was considered trustworthy enough to study at the seminary and rise through the church ranks. Early on, I had the feeling that something wasn't right, as interrogators became confessors. When I met Alexei Orlovsky, his words fell on fertile ground. He was laying the groundwork for a conspiracy, seeking out like-minded men like me, but ultimately failing. Yet he lit the fire in my soul which guided me to the right path. He admitted to being a member of the Catacomb Church. Today, his son carries on his legacy. Yakov is the head of a true Orthodox community of church dissidents. He and his followers have been persecuted by the authorities for opposing the Patriarchate. Some of his group members are former clerics who are privy to the Patriarchate's innermost secrets. The only person who can help you unravel the Oltersdorf mystery is Yakov."

"How do I contact him?"

7

Father Mikhail walked behind the edifice of the Trinity Cathedral, lit a Marlboro, and dialed a number on his cell phone. He took a few long pulls at the cigarette before the connection established. In a hushed voice, Mikhail spoke into the mouthpiece.

"The old man had a visitor. It was Constantine Sokolov. He's just left ... I tried my best to ward him off, but the old man came out to see him ... Yes, I know I was supposed to keep him sedated! He said he woke up because he had a vision. Can you believe it? My hands were tied ... No, I couldn't catch any of their conversation. The old man doesn't know that his room is wired, and yet they talked outside. I was out of earshot ... All right, I'll keep an eye on him until you get here. I concur, you should handle the issue yourself. At once."

8

Hong Kong

In the cavernous Arrivals hall of Hong Kong International Airport, an immense queue lined up for immigration control. Priding themselves on the airport's efficiency, the security staff dealt with the arriving passengers quickly. The queue started clearing in minutes. Awaiting his turn in the midst of the travelers, a man approached an immigration counter and presented his passport and a filled-out arrival card to the officer. The weary Chinese border official swiped the machine-readable passport through a scanner without looking up at its holder, a Mr. Calum McKinley, British national, dressed in a navy polo, slacks, and a baseball cap. In lieu of a stamp, the officer returned the passport with a landing slip: a strip of paper indicating Mr. McKinley's passport details, arrival date, and permitted stay in Hong Kong. The man snatched the passport—unceremoniously thrown back to him by the immigration officer atop the desk—and crossed the imaginary border to enter Hong Kong.

At an adjacent counter, Stacie Rose handed her Italian passport with a completed card to a different immigration officer. Her expression froze in a practiced smile, but her heart accelerated. The Chinese glanced up at her for a nerve-wracking moment. Back at the hotel, she'd spent several hours applying make-up to perfect her Federica Buonamano look. Ruby-red lipstick ripened her mouth, the liner tracing her lips just outside the natural edges to make them seem fuller. Highlights and contours reshaped her face as close as possible to the passport photo, adding a darker complexion. The cosmetic tricks created a dolled-up version of the woman she was impersonating, much more beautiful but recognizable nonetheless. The illusion was convincing enough.

Or so she hoped.

Oblivious to her extreme anxiety, the immigration officer resumed his mundane task without hesitation. Never bothering to compare her appearance against the photo, he couldn't possibly suspect a double. He placed the instantly-issued landing slip inside the passport and gave it back to her. Inwardly shaking, she muttered thanks, picked it up, and joined Eugene Sokolov at the Baggage Reclaim Hall.

The baseball cap clashed with Sokolov's clothes, but it offered the best option to conceal his rich hairline.

"I can't quite believe that we've made it," she said in a thrilled voice.

"You played it cool. I'm proud of you."

She smiled sheepishly. "What's our next step?"

"It's already late, so you'd better get some rest. This time, I've booked separate hotel rooms. I'll drop you off at the hotel and head over to the Russian church for a quick stake-out. This way, we can go after your pendant first thing in the morning, fully prepared."

"I have a better idea," she announced. "Let's check out this Russian church together. Right now, on our way to the hotel."

"Are you sure you're up for it?"

"I won't rest easy knowing that you're out there, alone in the night, risking your life for me."

"It's a routine scouting mission," he assured her. "Just a precaution."

"All the more reason for us to stick together. Besides, should we run into Father Mark, I know what he looks like and you don't."

"Okay," Sokolov agreed. "We'll make a detour, look around and plan for tomorrow."

Save for the Louis Vuitton, neither Sokolov nor Stacie carried any luggage. They marched through Customs via the green channel, unhindered. Outside the futuristic terminal, Sokolov hailed a taxi and told the cabbie to drive to Queen's Road. Stacie remembered reading somewhere that Queen's Road was the first street built in Hong Kong. The city's main commercial thoroughfare since the days of the early British colonists. How did a Russian church possibly belong there? Curiosity was getting the better of her.

When they reached their destination a half hour later, Stacie saw that no Russian church could fit into the surroundings.

Queen's Road West was one of the four sections comprising the main street, lined with high-rise buildings and shops. The red-bodied, white-roofed taxi cruised amid a steady traffic of sedans and lorries. Storefronts flashed with boisterous neon signs in Chinese and English. Pedestrians bustled along busy sidewalks.

Indeed, the church was nowhere in sight, which left Stacie even more puzzled when the cab pulled over at a narrow intersection with the merchant-packed Possession Street.

The bespectacled cabbie pointed a finger at the office building. "Two-Twelve, Queens Road West."

Incredulous, Stacie stepped out into the hot and humid Asian night. She stood in front of a blocky 1980's-style tower, numbering 26 floors. A sign read, *Arion Commercial Center.*

"Did you get the address right?" she asked Sokolov, who joined her in the street.

"The church is in fact an office on the seventh floor, according to the listing. Unit 701. It's registered as the St. Peter and St. Paul Orthodox Church. The office is shared with some Russian Language Center."

"A false front?" It explained Father Mark's businesslike attire and emphasized his cynicism. Even after everything she'd gone through, finding the church to be nothing more than leased space inside a commercial high-rise struck her as a farce.

"Could be a dead end," Sokolov said. "We might as well set out for the hotel."

The taxi driver was shouting at them angrily in Chinese.

"No," Stacie said. She scanned the lit windows of the seventh floor. "There's someone inside. Come on, we can't back away now."

Sokolov paid the fare and the cab sped away.

"Let's go," he said, leading the way inside Arion Commercial Center.

From the deserted lobby, they took the cargo elevator to the seventh floor. They exited the elevator into a narrow, tile-floored hallway. Closed doors loomed on either side of the stretching corridor. Stacie went after Sokolov across the deathly-quiet hallway.

He stopped at the door labeled: **701** – *St. Peter and St. Paul Orthodox Church – Russian Language Center.*

Stacie held her breath, straining to pick up any sound from beyond the door, but heard nothing.

Sokolov motioned for Stacie to stay back as he approached the office door. He wrapped his fingers around the doorknob and twisted gently. It wouldn't turn. The door was locked.

Sokolov strode to the end of the hallway and returned with a fire extinguisher in his hands. The silence erupted with a sudden burst of violent force. Swinging the fire extinguisher downward, he battered the doorknob, smashing the lock, and kicked the door in. A step behind him, Stacie followed Sokolov as he stormed into the office. Once inside, she found herself staring down the barrel of a gun.

9

Mark opened the fireproof safe and transferred the codebook, his Russian passport, a cash bundle and a sheaf of documents to his briefcase.

Dread had been coursing in Mark's veins since the call from Phuket. Unable to reach Song for several hours, he had assumed the worst. His growing premonition, fueled by vodka, had prompted him to return to the Arion Commercial Center and alter his schedule. He had to leave Hong Kong urgently. He couldn't afford to wait until tomorrow. Something had gone terribly wrong on Billionaire Island, he became certain of it. He couldn't risk the Oltersdorf codebook!

He extracted the last item, a Type 54 pistol known as the Black Star—the Chinese copy of the 7.62 mm Tokarev TT-33. As a standard-issue PLA handgun, the Black Star remained highly popular in the illegal arms market of Hong Kong. He loaded a full clip and swung the gun around the office. Orthodox icons adorned the office walls. He aimed the gun at the image of Christ across the empty room.

"Not even You can stop me," he told the Messiah.

Abruptly, the door crashed open and a man entered Office 701, together with a woman dressed in white like an angel. Mark leveled the Black Star at her.

Stacie Rose. It couldn't be her, could it? Yet there she was, not an apparition born from alcoholic delirium but flesh and blood.

You're supposed to be dead, he thought, *and I'll put that right.*

He squeezed the trigger.

Sokolov unleashed a jet of white spray from the powder-based fire extinguisher. It hit the man's face in a puffy cloud. Groaning in pain as the powder burned his eyes, he fired a blind shot into the ceiling, arms flailing. Sokolov swung the fire extinguisher across his face, smashing the nose with an audible crunch. The man's head snapped sideways. A torrent of blood gushed from the broken nose as he toppled, clutching his face and dropping the handgun. Sokolov kicked the gun away.

Whimpering, the man crawled on all fours and propped himself against the nearest wall. Sokolov surveyed the office, which appeared devoid of furnishings apart from a few icons hanging on the walls and a digital-dial steel safe hidden behind a folding screen. An open briefcase rested atop the safe.

"Is that him?" Sokolov asked Stacie.

"Yes," she said, picking up the pistol off the floor. "He's the one who attacked me on the plane and stole my pendant. Father Mark."

Mark sobbed, his nose bent grotesquely, his face smeared white and red with a mixture of blood and dry chemicals. Sokolov raised the fire extinguisher.

"I hope you can answer a few questions, Mark, or whatever your name is. A couple of your buddies died before I could ask them."

"No, please! Don't kill me! I'll do anything you want!"

"You'll do anything *she* wants. But I can't vouch for her actions. She may shoot you even before I'm done with you."

Mark's bloodshot eyes grew wide in horror at the sight of Stacie pointing the gun square at his chest.

"I beg you! Have mercy! By all that's holy!"

"Where's the pendant?" Stacie asked.

"Inside the briefcase."

"And the codebook?"

"It's there, all there!"

Going through the contents of the briefcase, Stacie found both. She clasped the pendant around her neck. Then she held up the codebook.

"What's so important about it? What secret did my great-great-grandfather possess that could be worth killing for today?"

Mark clenched his jaw.

"Answer her."

Mark blinked rapidly.

"I don't know the details. I swear by God!"

"God? I'll let Him be your judge," said Sokolov as he stepped toward Mark, his weapon raised with apparent intent to maim or kill.

Mark held up his hand defensively. "No! Stop! All right, listen. The Oltersdorf notebook contains information that will swing the balance of power in Siberia. The Patriarchate has been after it for years, and so have the Chinese."

"What interest do the Chinese have in it?" Sokolov asked.

"It's a bargaining chip for the next round of negotiations. As you know, the economic sanctions imposed by the West have placed the Kremlin under immense pressure. The Russian economy is failing as oil revenues are dropping. Cash-strapped, the Russian oligarchs have turned to China for financial backing. The Chinese know how desperate the Russians are, and they want to get maximum advantage. Beijing wants access to Siberia's natural resources. Perhaps even the concession of certain territories."

"Why would the Patriarchate act on behalf of the Russian oligarchs?"

"Because the Patriarch himself is one of the biggest oligarchs. He controls the Russian alcohol and tobacco markets, and has a stake in the diamond industry, oil and gas, you name it. And he may hold the key to Russia's future as a country."

"How come?"

"Over the last few decades, the Patriarchate has been hunting for a hidden source of unimaginable wealth. Lost treasure, located somewhere in Siberia and currently worth at least 200 billion U.S. dollars. It is known that the treasure's exact location is encrypted in the Oltersdorf notebook."

Two hundred *billion*? Sokolov contemplated the figure. It was enough to turn the tables. No wonder the Chinese wanted to thwart any attempts to obtain it.

"What role does Saveliy Frolov play?"

"He's in charge of the so-called Order of Holy Orthodox Knights. It's a front for clandestine operations. For example, the Patriarchate uses it as an unofficial channel to deal with the North Koreans."

"To what end?"

"The Oltersdorf notebook is just a part of the picture, a contingency plan in the operation they are running. The Patriarch and Frolov have devised a scheme to break away from Chinese influence completely. Once triggered, it's a gamble they believe they cannot lose. Operation Temple."

"And what exactly is Operation Temple supposed to trigger?"

Grimacing through the pain, Mark twisted his mouth in a crooked smile.

"A doomsday event."

"What the hell are you talking about?"

"An unprecedented act of terrorism."

"What's the target?"

"When it comes to Church matters, look no further than the Holy Land."

"Israel? This is madness," Stacie said.

"Far from it," said Mark. "Using the North Koreans, they want to supply the Iranians with the required weapons—and set them up, incidentally. The attack will throw the Middle East into turmoil and Iran will get the blame. Oil prices will soar and Moscow will gain leeway in the talks with Beijing, especially with that extra 200 billion from the Oltersdorf affair."

"The risk is insane. What if the terrorist plot is exposed, and the instigators of the attack are traced back to Moscow? Russia will become a pariah. The leaders of every country will turn away, including the Chinese. We'll face total international isolation."

Mark nodded slowly. "Exactly. What better way to keep the populace in check than the threat of a new world war? Yes, Russia will be ostracized from the civilized world, but isolationism is the very objective. A new Iron Curtain, a siege mentality, an indoctrinated 'us-against-them' worldview which is the only way to keep power in an impoverished country, suppressing all dissent. We're fully committed to going the North Korean route, albeit with a twist—an Iranian-style theocracy. The Patriarch will be proclaimed as the new national leader and the Patriarchate will govern the country. Those in power will retain their positions forever. Again, the 200 billion will come in handy until the West eventually recognizes the new regime. The wheels are in motion. And there's nothing you or your Aussie whore can do about it!"

Sokolov bludgeoned him.

10

At the Trinity Lavra, Father Mikhail peered into the cold darkness of the night. He waited for his rendezvous outside the sprawling, three-storied baroque building which housed the monks' cells. A shadow moved across the courtyard, the man's stealthy approach startling Mikhail as a voice sounded behind him.

"Is he inside?"

The voice was as cold as the surrounding darkness.

"Yes. He's in his cell, sedated."

Mikhail turned toward the man, who was of average height and build, wearing jeans and a bomber jacket. He had the kind of appearance that never stood out in any environment, a chameleon-like quality to stay unnoticed. He went by different names, including Herman, Imran and Victor, but nobody knew his real identity.

In the mid-1990s, an entire FSB hit team had rebelled against their boss, refusing to assassinate a Russian businessman. They'd chosen to stick their neck out rather than play any part in a political conspiracy. Wary of that incident, FSB Director Saveliy Frolov employed a hitman loyal to him personally, and him alone. Not bound by any rules, the assassin carried out the dirtiest jobs for Frolov, and continued to do so even after his master had formally left the FSB. Victor was a former Spetsnaz officer like Father Mikhail himself. And now Mikhail was assisting the hitman on a job that couldn't get any dirtier.

Mikhail ascended the stairs to the second floor and arrived at the door of Ilia's cell. He unlocked it with his own key. Victor trained a penlight on the Spartan interior of the cell, which comprised a simple cot, a wooden chair, and a desk stacked with books. A prone figure occupied the cot, one arm dangling over the edge of the thin mattress. A large crucifix hung on the wall over the bed.

Ilia lay senseless.

Together, Victor and Mikhail dragged the old man from his cot, across the floor and down the stairs, and placed him in a wheelchair which Mikhail had brought from the monastery's medical unit. Then they wheeled Ilia outside, all the way across the main plaza and through the Holy Gates.

Victor's nondescript gray Hyundai sedan was waiting in the parking lot just beyond the ancient stone walls of the Lavra, illuminated by streetlights.

Beads of perspiration rolled down Mikhail's face as he helped haul Ilia's body into the trunk. The old man moaned as Victor slammed it shut.

They drove in silence, the hitman and the priest, both former GRU officers, now doing what they did best. The Hyundai reached the outskirts of Sergiev Posad. Once out of town, they headed south-west, to a wooded area. As he turned to a gravel road cutting through a forest, Victor stopped the car at the roadside and killed the engine. Mikhail could hear Ilia's muffled groans emanating from inside the trunk.

The two of them got out of the car. The surrounding scenery looked forlorn, with skeletal trees and no other motorists in sight. Victor opened the Hyundai's trunk.

"Who are you? What do you want from me?" Ilia shouted through the darkness.

"You know the answers to both questions," said the assassin.

"Herman? No! No!"

The assassin swung a fist, slugging Ilia in the face. As the old man cried out in pain, the hitman grabbed him by the shoulders and pulled him out of the trunk, dragging him into the dense blackness behind rows of trees.

Mikhail lit a cigarette. Halfway through it, he heard the first screams. The interrogation could drag on for a while, he knew.

He crushed the cigarette butt with his foot and flicked his lighter to ignite the next one. It glowed faintly in the night which was only broken by screams. He watched it burn while the screams intensified, melding into one blood-curdling cry.

He quashed a wave of nausea, but even more sickening than the old man's screaming was the total silence that fell abruptly afterwards. His fingers trembled slightly as he finished the cigarette. He'd grown too soft since his retirement from the GRU.

He noticed that a sliver of the rising sun, as fiery as his dying cigarette stub, had rendered a gray hue to the dark sky.

A red dawn was breaking.

Clear in the brighter light, Victor emerged from the forest, his bomber jacket splattered with blood.

Mikhail had grown too soft and too slack. He never saw the shot coming as Frolov's hitman put a bullet through his skull.

PART IV

1

SIBERIA

Inferno. It was hell on earth as a gigantic column of fire gushed from the ground, rising a hundred meters into the sky. Even standing four kilometers away, Eduard Malkovich felt nothing but awe as he observed the colossal flame burning amid the snow-covered Siberian wasteland.

In a blowout at one of the largest gas wells, the fountain of natural gas had burst out at a pressure of 300 atmospheres, catching fire and incinerating the drill tower. The blowout had occurred 465 days ago, the gargantuan torch devouring 12 million cubic meters of gas per day.

The resulting heat was so ferocious that it made the fire unapproachable within several hundred meters, charring the permafrost around it and roaring with a thunderous din. The sheer force of the blowout sent vibrations across the icy plain. Here in Yakutia, on the fringes of the Arctic Circle, polar twilight would normally descend in winter, shrouding the area in darkness. In the vicinity of the blowout, however, the blazing inferno brightened the sky in a shimmering haze as if it were broad daylight.

Over the last fifteen months, all attempts to quench the blowout by conventional means had proved ineffective. The gas gusher would keep on burning for years to come—unless Eduard Malkovich succeeded in stopping the uncontrolled release. And he would. Today. In just over an hour. To do it, he put his own life on the line.

Malkovich treaded over the frozen soil toward a low structure built from concrete. The distant fire reflected in the transparent faceplate of his hazmat suit. The suit was capable of withstanding extreme conditions, but the air temperature hovered around the

-20 degrees Celsius mark, well above the average high of -50 that would set in in a few weeks.

At the entrance, Malkovich was greeted by a pair of FSB sentries guarding the structure. Each wore a green camo uniform and a sheepskin hat with ear-flaps, called *ushanka*. FSB troops patrolled the area along the four-kilometer radius outside the blowout. Farther away, the perimeter eight kilometers away from the blowout was secured by special police forces flown in from Moscow, just like their FSB counterparts. Such airtight security might have seemed excessive. The part of East Siberia known as Yakutia had a population of under a million people, despite being greater in size than Argentina. The remote northern areas of Yakutia were especially deserted. Hundreds of kilometers of forbidding terrain separated the blowout from the nearest village. But Malkovich deemed the defensive measures reasonable as far as his job was concerned.

Inside the structure, he found a team of technicians, clad in yellow coveralls. They were buzzing as they went through final preparations, paying no heed to Malkovich when he entered. The source of their attention lay positioned on a transport dolly in front of a bank of testing equipment hooked to it by wires. The object was a cylindrical tube, 85 centimeters in diameter and three meters long. The black casing glinted in the glare of overhead lamps. It was a 20-kiloton nuclear explosive device.

Content that he'd glimpsed the fruit of his labor for one last time, Malkovich exited the Assembly Building and made his way back to the Control Center, an identical structure located next to it. He heard the thumping of rotor blades as choppers circled above for a final inspection of the danger zone. A cargo helicopter was descending to touch down behind the Control Center, on stand-by to evacuate personnel in case of emergency.

Malkovich removed his headgear, revealing his weathered, mustached face as he stepped from the cold into the confines of the Control Center.

"Everything is going according to plan," Malkovich reported to a senior man dressed in similar protective coveralls. The man cut a short and rotund figure, his face clean-shaven and wrinkled. Curly gray hair surrounded the bald spot on his head. His name was Vladlen Zeldin. In their quest for progress, the Soviets had fought with reactionary Christian names, coming up with new ones. Vladlen was an initialism which stood for *Vladimir Lenin*. Both Zeldin and Malkovich worked at the Institute of

Experimental Physics based in Sarov, a town 400 kilometers south-east of Moscow. True to his name, Vladlen Zeldin was a Soviet stalwart, a man who had spent his entire career in a top-ranking position at the Soviet Los Alamos. Semi-retired, he now acted as the younger man's supervisor and immediate boss.

The twelfth-century town of Sarov had been famous for its medieval monastery. After the Revolution, the Bolsheviks had shut the Sarov Monastery down, killing the monks, and converted it into an NKVD prison. Later, Sarov had become a restricted area for top-secret nuclear research. The entire town had vanished from every map. The defiled churches of the Monastery still stood next to the classified facilities.

To quote Vladlen Zeldin's article from a 1988 issue of *Scientific Atheism*: "*The use of atomic energy is regarded as Man's triumph over Nature. Nuclear physics has given Man the ability to part seas and blow up mountains at will. But to be more precise, Man has defeated God, leaving no place for religion. Sarov, pried from medieval darkness to serve all Mankind, is the biggest testament to such conquest.*"

Apparently, though, Zeldin's attitude toward organized religion had improved as of late. Making a U-turn, he'd bridged the gap with the Moscow Patriarchate, even taking an honorary position at some sort of Orthodox organization. Oddities accompanied old age, Malkovich figured. Perhaps it was just as well. After the success of the current mission, Malkovich would reap all the rewards, push Zeldin closer to full retirement and usurp his position at the Institute.

"The explosion is scheduled at 10:00 sharp," Malkovich added.

"When the countdown approaches zero, make sure you're standing on your tiptoes to avoid spine damage from the quake," Zeldin joked. His eyes narrowed slyly. He was in good humor. Days like this didn't come about very often.

"Any other valuable experience you can share, Professor?"

Zeldin peered at the fiery vortex four kilometers away through twin windows, tiny slits in the thick concrete walls of the Control Center.

"If you see a huge mushroom cloud breaking the surface, run for the helicopter." The old man chuckled, baring nicotine-stained teeth. During the blast, the windows would be closed by metal shutters, they both knew, but if the underground explosion ended in disaster, they could do little about it. "Don't worry, Eduard, your calculations are flawless. Your team has done a fine job. I was there in 1972 when we applied the same method in Ukraine, outside Kharkov. Similarly, we drilled a directional hole, two and a half kilometers long. It slanted downward until it reached the gas well. Then the explosive device was lowered down the hole and detonated. The only reason we failed to seal the gusher was because the nuclear charge wasn't powerful enough at under four kilotons. In your case, twenty kilotons should be enough to cause a subterranean soil shift that will block the gas well from the source of the fire. Over the years, I've dealt with devices of thirty and fifty kilotons as well, but you realize that there are some things I can't tell you."

Malkovich nodded. He himself had signed a 15-year non-disclosure agreement relating to all information on the blowout.

A commotion outside the Control Center became audible. The whine of helicopter rotors intensified. Added to it was the rumbling diesel of a heavy KAMAZ truck. Sharp cracks of gunfire chattered above the engine noise. Malkovich bolted to the door and pulled it open. He couldn't believe his eyes.

"What the hell is going on?" he muttered.

The KAMAZ truck was towing the bomb-laden dolly out of the Assembly Building, far earlier than expected. And the truck wasn't moving along the intended route to the slanting hole, or even in the direction of the blowout. Instead, it was heading toward the cargo chopper which had just landed. Its rear loading ramp opened and soldiers in white camouflage, armed with AK rifles, swarmed out like a pack of rats. They charged into the Assembly Building, facing no resistance from a lone FSB guard. If anything, the sentry was assisting the invaders, *letting* them inside.

Then Malkovich saw the body of the truck driver in yellow coveralls lying sprawled in the snow, spewing blood. He realized that it wasn't his technician, but rather the second FSB guard driving the truck, towing the nuclear device to the waiting Mi-8 helicopter.

A staccato of gunfire boomed inside the Assembly Building, mixed with anguished cries.

One of the specialists managed to escape from the slaughterhouse. Frantically, he ran outside before a trio of chasing attackers blasted him from their AKs, splattering gore over the pristine snow.

"Everything is going according to plan," Zeldin's voice sounded behind Malkovich. "My plan, that is, not yours. But you must realize there are certain things I can't tell you."

Malkovich pivoted, eyes wide in disbelief.

"Have you lost your mind, Professor?"

The force of the burning gas gusher was so immense that the fire produced low-frequency acoustic waves, well below the limit of human hearing. Although inaudible, the emitted infrasound traveled great distances and impacted the nervous system. Prolonged exposure to infrasonic waves caused feelings of anxiety, fear, revulsion, sorrow and aggression, and could lead to insanity. That could explain the FSB guards going berserk, Malkovich thought. But none of the winter-camouflaged troops looked like they were suffering from nervous breakdowns. And who the hell were they, anyway?

No, it was a pre-planned attack. Zeldin's involvement disgusted Malkovich.

Vladlen Zeldin spoke in a measured, condescending tone.

"Of all people, Eduard, you should be aware that the Soviet nuclear program owed its success much less to physicists than it did to spies. Scientists couldn't have built the bomb without the theft of atomic secrets from the West, hence it was the NKVD chief, Beria, who was in charge of the Soviet nuclear program. A man of my rank is always involved in espionage, not research. Shame that true scientists like you must take the fall, but there's no way around it."

"You're stealing the nuclear explosive device," Malkovich blurted. It was more statement than question.

"I knew from the start that you'd object to it, so your team had to be eliminated. Besides, it's the North Koreans stealing it. At least, everything should point to them in the event of a blowback. Plausible deniability requires maximum carnage. I'm sorry I had to sacrifice you. Rest assured, you're dying for a great cause."

Malkovich turned around to see the three assailants closing in on him. The ear-flaps of their winter hats partially concealed their faces, but they looked Asian. One of the North Koreans trained his AK at Malkovich and it spat a hot burst of slugs. Searing pain bored through his abdomen. Gasping, he collapsed over the threshold of the Control Center. His blood pooled on the icy ground. Indeed, he was dying.

He had never envisaged such a fate for himself. Mentally, he'd accepted the professional risk of exposure to radiation, perhaps even a lethal dose, though he never dwelled on such a possibility.

But this? Collateral damage in a false-flag operation. It was a sick joke, but he wasn't laughing.

He pressed his hands against the punctures in a vain attempt to stop the squirting blood. His vision clouded.

"Finish him off," Zeldin ordered.

Another volley blasted, only this time it didn't hit Malkovich.

Vladlen Zeldin crashed down next to him, shot dead, off to meet the God he'd supposedly beaten. Zeldin's face froze in a death mask of surprised horror. Having played his role in the conspiracy, he'd become expendable. The joke was on him, after all.

Malkovich's mouth twisted into a pained smirk just as bullets ripped his throat, blood gurgling.

Neither of them had started the day expecting to die at the hands of North Korean killers.

The last thing Eduard Malkovich ever heard was the thumping of helicopter rotors as the big Mi-8 lifted off, silhouetted in the sky by the distant burn of the gas blowout. Onboard, the transport chopper carried a deadly group of North Korean passengers and a 20-kiloton nuclear cargo. The corpses left behind marked the start of a blood-drenched race across the Siberian wasteland.

2

The man exiting the school building wore a navy-colored wool overcoat and a matching fedora hat. Tall and wiry, he carried an air of dignity about him, his movements filled with poise. With a neatly-trimmed salt-and-pepper beard, he appeared to be in his late forties or early fifties. His dark eyes were constantly alert.

"Excuse me, are you Yakov Orlovsky?"

"At your service. How may I help you, young man?"

"My name is Constantine Sokolov. I believe we have a mutual friend—Ilia."

"Oh yes, I remember. Father Ilia spoke highly of you when we last met a couple of years ago."

They walked together down Prechistenka, a sixteenth-century street which linked the Novodevichy Convent with the Kremlin. The façades of historical houses still lining the street bore traces of a bygone era, evoking memories of the eradicated Russian aristocracy. Few pedestrians milled about on the sidewalks, enabling a private conversation.

"You're a historian, if I'm not mistaken?" asked Orlovsky.

"Indeed, I am. It's part of the reason why I'm here."

"There's a vacancy at the school where I teach. Perhaps you might be interested?"

Constantine smiled sardonically. "Funny that you mentioned it. I got fired from a college teaching job. Thanks, but I wanted to ask you about something else."

"History is a dangerous profession in this country. I'm so sorry about your layoff."

"No worries. Frankly, I was surprised to hear about *your* profession."

"Art teacher by day, icon painter by night."

"And also, the head of a Christian community defying the Patriarchate," Constantine noted.

"I'm not on the winning side, but with God's help nothing is ever lost. We call ourselves the Brotherhood of True Believers. Like the early Christians hiding from the Pharisees two thousand years ago, we meet covertly. To avoid detection, the venue must keep changing, so the Brotherhood leases several properties scattered around Moscow."

"Safe houses?"

"You could put it that way. It takes spycraft to fight spies. The safe houses leave much to be desired, but one has to make do with whatever's available. Last Sunday, it was a room inside a Khrushchev-era apartment block, a stone's throw away from the old KGB prison in Lefortovo. The symbolism is ironic, isn't it? Conducting religious services in some crumbling old apartment does feel wrong, but we view it as God's test of our resolve. Our churches have been taken away from us, but not our faith. I'm inviting you to join."

"I appreciate your trust, Father Yakov."

"Please, call me Yakov Alexeich, like my students do. If Father Ilia trusts you, that's more than enough for me. We need more good men to keep the light shining through the darkness."

An enormous golden-domed edifice loomed ahead. It was the fake Cathedral of Christ the Savior, erected after the nominal fall of communism. The original had been destroyed in 1931 by Stalin with a view to construct the Palace of the Soviets in its place—a monstrous 400-meter-tall tower of communist worship. Fortunately, the abomination had never been built beyond its gigantic 160-meter-wide basement. The basement now housed a commercial center, with the fake cathedral slapped atop it in lieu of the Lenin monument which should have crowned the completed palace, a cheap knockoff which only bore an outward resemblance to the original. It occurred to Constantine that the fake church had served the intended purpose of the Palace of the Soviets: a monument to the triumph of evil. It was there, inside the fake cathedral that the Russian clerical hierarchy had signed the act of surrender to the fake church.

"So, what is it that you want to talk to me about?" Orlovsky asked.

"Peter Oltersdorf," replied Constantine. "Do you know anything about the contents of the Oltersdorf papers?"

"I do. Perhaps more than anyone else. But I'm not sure this is the right time and place for such a sensitive topic. It's a long story. I don't even know where to start."

"Please, Yakov Alexeich, at least give me a clue."

"Very well. You're a historian, after all. How much do you know about Admiral Kolchak?"

A crimson flower bloomed in Yakov Orlovsky's chest, splashing blood to the sound of a gunshot. Orlovsky gaped in mute shock. Stumbling, he clutched at Constantine's leather jacket before another bullet tore into his shoulder. A terrifying rasp issued from the throat of the dying man. His knees buckled, his body going limp as he held onto Constantine for support. A third slug pierced Orlovsky's temple. As Orlovsky's dead body slumped against Constantine, he lowered the sagging weight to the ground.

Overcoming his stupor, Constantine faced the direction of the gunfire.

A Hyundai sedan pulled level. The driver was shooting through the open window.

He saw the muzzle flash a split second earlier than his mind registered the agonizing pain in his left arm. Warm, sticky blood trickled down his forearm and oozed through his fingers as he clamped the wound with his right hand.

He had to flee. But as he spun away and broke into a sprint, a sizzling slug penetrated his left side. He staggered, pressing against the wall of the nearest house and slipping into an alley.

He ran as fast as his legs carried him, fueled by adrenaline but leaking blood. He dared not look back, knowing that the assassin would be in hot pursuit. At least one shooter sat behind the wheel of the gray Hyundai: there could be others closing in on him. Who were they? How many? He anticipated danger lurking behind every corner, and evil intent in every figure moving toward him. But the people around him reacted to his plight with cold-hearted indifference, ignoring his gunshot wounds or quickening their step to keep a safe distance. Not a single person tried to offer help. You could get shot in broad daylight and nobody would give a damn.

Constantine darted through the twisting alleys, exiting the maze of old buildings a few hundred meters away from the scene of Orlovsky's murder. He found himself right in front of the mock Cathedral of Christ the Savior. He quickly changed direction, jogging alongside the Soviet-built cyclopean pedestal it rested upon, circumventing it. He dashed past a flock of tourists across the pedestrian Patriarshy Bridge which spanned the Moskva River. The ominous shape of the cathedral receded behind him.

Like in a bad dream, he felt as if its evil presence was tugging him back, sucking the life out of him.

The ravaging pain sapped his strength. He had to act on instinct alone. Police or ambulance sirens could prove just as deadly to him as another gun blast. For all he knew, the assassin was connected with the Patriarchate, and hence the FSB. He couldn't let them find him and finish the job. Public transportation was out of the question for the same reason. He had nowhere to go. Heading back home he might walk straight into an ambush. He reached into his pocket for his phone, not knowing if there was anyone he could call. Gene was probably still on a mission in Asia. But as he fished out the phone, any hope of getting help ebbed away. A round hole gaped in the middle of the cracked touchscreen, perforated by the slug which had hit his side. He tossed away the dead device. At least they wouldn't be able to use the phone to track him.

Without the phone, his front jacket pocket should have been empty but he felt that it contained another object. Something that wasn't supposed to be there. Warily, he fished out a key ring holding a couple of door keys. Yakov Orlovsky must have slipped it inside his pocket as he died, Constantine realized. He had never seen the key ring before, and had no idea why Orlovsky—

The safe house.

Even in death, Orlovsky had given him a lifeline.

Reaching the embankment on the other side of the river, Constantine stopped at a curb and scanned the traffic. Hailing a cab carried risk, as many taxi drivers were former or active FSB men. He needed to find an illegal taxi operating without a license. Moscow was rife with unlicensed cars for hire, but none seemed to be around when he needed one urgently. It was down to pure luck to catch one cruising within a few blocks of the Kremlin, and Constantine spent a few minutes signaling for any vehicle to stop.

His limbs became weak. He could no longer think clearly. He expected the gray Hyundai to appear from nowhere at any moment. The area was crammed with security cameras which covered every inch of every street. If they had access to video feeds, his pursuers would spot him soon. The assassin would dispatch him with ease.

Fear mounted as cars sped by. Then, abruptly, a beat-up Ford hatchback pulled over, tires squealing as it braked. Its sole occupant was an olive-skinned man, perhaps a Tajik immigrant. He rolled down the window and stuck his head out.

"Where to?"

"Southeast District."

"Hop in."

A wave of relief washed over Constantine as he climbed into the rear of the dark green hatchback.

The car eased back into the flow of traffic. The driver glanced at Constantine in the rearview mirror. As soon as he noticed his passenger's condition, his mouth twisted in an angry scowl.

"Hey, is that blood? I don't want any trouble!"

"Neither do I, so I won't tell anyone that you don't have a meter running." Constantine winced in pain. "What's your name?"

"Waheed."

"How much do you want, Waheed?"

"Two hundred."

"What?" Constantine asked, confused.

"Not rubles, by Allah! Two hundred bucks. American. And another two hundred to wash the car."

Four hundred dollars sounded steep, but Constantine wasn't going to bargain over the price of his survival. He reached inside the jacket for his wallet, glad that he kept his savings in the U.S. currency. He counted off four Ben Franklin portraits and shoved a single bill into Waheed's outstretched palm.

"Here's a hundred. I'll give you the rest when we get there."

"May Allah reward you and strike your enemies!"

"Thanks for the wishes, but I'd prefer a first aid kit at the moment. You got one?"

"It's behind the passenger seat."

"Now that's what I call top-class service," Constantine muttered as he found the bag in the storage space at the back, along with a bottle of mineral water. He grabbed both and rummaged the first aid kit. First, he popped a couple of painkillers, washing the pills down with a gulp of water. Then he picked out the items he could use to treat his wounds and stem the bleeding: gauze pads, bandages, antiseptics, adhesive tape, and scissors.

"Southeast, you say?" asked Waheed. "Which address, exactly?"

"Lefortovo Prison."

"Man, you turning yourself in or something?"

"Yeah. Something like that. Just drive, Waheed."

"Okay, whatever you say, chief."

3

Out of caution, Waheed stopped the Ford a few blocks away from the prison, which was fine with Constantine. He handed his Muslim driver the remaining three hundred dollars and got off. His legs felt wobbly. He retrieved the keychain and glanced at the label attached to it. Only the house and apartment numbers were written on the label—*12, 8*—without the actual street address. Constantine hoped he could manage to locate the right house. Only a few Khrushchev-era buildings still existed within walking distance of the prison. The majority of the 1960s slums had already been demolished all around Moscow. He'd stumble on his destination, eventually. However, the stabbing pain in his left side and upper arm reminded Constantine that he couldn't waste time on a lengthy search.

Soon enough, he spotted a dilapidated five-storied apartment block with a matching number, 12. The ugly, concrete-paneled building had the soulless look of communist architecture and all the charm of prison barracks. This particular structure appeared as dead as the Soviet Union. Cracked paint had peeled off the front door. The interior was just as shabby, Constantine saw as he entered. Dim light emanated from a single light bulb, barely illuminating the graffiti-stained walls. At four apartments per level, number 8 had to be the last unit on the second floor. There was no elevator, so Constantine took the stairs. Finding the right door, he pressed the buzzer to check if anyone was inside. He waited for any rustle to sound from within but he only heard his own breathing, heavy from the exertion of his ordeal. He inserted the key and twisted it. The door lock clicked, opening. He turned the handle, pulled the door ajar, slipped inside, slammed the door shut and locked it again with the key.

He felt disoriented at first, surrounded by darkness. After the overwhelming stench which had permeated the stairway, he noticed that the apartment smelled clean. In fact, he sensed a strange yet distinct scent, but he couldn't quite put his finger on what it was. His hand searched for the light switch. As he turned the lights on, he discovered the source of the peculiar odor.

The farthest wall of the living room formed an improvised iconostasis, with rows of framed icons hanging from floor to ceiling. The smell of incense lingered in the air after a recent service, Constantine realized. The only pieces of furniture were a conference table and several chairs arranged before a triptych depicting Christ's Crucifixion, the Resurrection and the Harrowing of Hell. The icons must have been painted by Orlovsky himself. The divine images transported Constantine's mind away from the reeking old building he was in, making him forget about his own pain and suffering. He mouthed a prayer, asking the Lord to rest the soul of His devout servant, Yakov Orlovsky. Then he pressed together the tips of his first three blood-smeared fingers and blessed himself with the sign of the cross.

True to typical design, the apartment measured thirty meters. From the living room acting as a church, Constantine proceeded into a tiny cubicle furnished with a couch and a desk. A landline phone rested atop the desk. He picked the handset off the cradle and heard the hum of a dial tone.

He had no room for error. He assumed that his brother's phone was tapped. All the communications of his friends and acquaintances could be monitored. Constantine's call would get flagged immediately. He couldn't risk revealing his location to the assassin and also putting another innocent life in danger.

Constantine remembered that Gene's friend had boasted about having an untraceable phone number. A tech wizard like Pavel Netto certainly possessed the expertise for it. If he could afford to make just one call, he had to call Pavel. He raked his memory for the number, but it eluded him. As a hacker, Pavel had fixed it to something simple in order to show off.

The frustration was killing him as much as the wounds. Finally, it hit him. The first few digits of Pi. Mentally, he thanked his math schoolteacher.

He punched in the sequence and waited for the call to go through.

"Yeah, who is it? How do you know this number?"

"Pavel, it's Constantine. Where's Gene?"

"Hi, dude. His plane has just touched down at the airbase."

"I need him. I'm in pretty bad shape but there's nobody I can trust."

"What's the matter?"

"I've been shot. I'm hiding at a safe house."

"Oh, damn! Where are you? I'll let Gene know at once. You hang in there, buddy."

Constantine gave him the address. "And Pavel, tell Gene that the attack is connected with the name he mentioned. Oltersdorf. I think I know the secret."

Constantine put the phone back in its cradle, drawing out a long breath. Now he could only wait for the arrival of reinforcements. He paced the room but after a few steps it suddenly started spinning around him. Swaying from the vertigo, he sank onto the couch, which seemed to shake under his body. Then he blacked out.

4

The Ilyushin Il-76 aircraft taxied off the runway of the EMERCOM airbase outside Moscow, having completed a twenty-hour haul to Hong Kong and back.

As they got off the plane, Sokolov draped his heavy parka over Stacie's shoulders to shield her from the cold. The warm clothing they'd picked up in Hong Kong proved inadequate against icy gusts and flurries of snow.

A Land Rover raced across the tarmac toward them. It braked sharply, skidding in front of Sokolov and Stacie. Behind the wheel, a harried Pavel Netto motioned for them to get inside the vehicle. Sokolov opened the rear passenger door for Stacie and sat next to her, surrounded by waves of hot air wafting from the car's heater.

Netto hit the accelerator, steering the Land Rover in the direction of a helipad where a Eurocopter EC145 was already revving up, rotor blades whipping the air.

Their pre-arranged plan didn't include a helicopter.

"What's going on?" Sokolov asked.

"Gene, we have an emergency."

"What is it?"

"Your brother. Somebody shot him."

The news hit him like a punch in the gut. Sokolov steeled himself.

"Is Constantine alive?" he demanded.

Netto spoke in a grave voice. "He's wounded. That's all I know. He called me from some sort of a hideout a couple of minutes ago."

"Do you know where he is?"

"Yeah, he told me. I considered sending in a medical team, but it could do more harm than good. Constantine said something about a secret he'd uncovered. He sounded paranoid. He doesn't trust anyone. Things can go haywire if someone other than you shows up. Not that I can blame him. We don't know what condition he's in. Whoever attacked him may still be out there, waiting to pounce on a mistake. We'll make it quicker on our own by chopper. In any case, I had to notify you first."

"You did the right thing. Let's get moving," Sokolov said. Then he turned to Stacie. "I hate to leave you like this. My friend Sergei will take you to the Australian Embassy immediately. Don't worry, you'll be safe."

"No," she protested. "Your brother risked his life because of me. If someone tried to kill him, it's my fault, don't you understand?"

"Stacie, don't blame yourself—"

"I'm going with you. I owe as much both to you and your brother. I might be able to help. My father is a doctor, I've learned enough from him to be useful."

Sokolov had no desire to argue. "Alright. And ... thanks."

"You were there for me, Eugene, and we'll stay together no matter what," she said.

Seconds later, they were airborne once more, this time aboard the Eurocopter.

5

The Eurocopter swooped down, arriving at an EMERCOM rapid-response facility in east Moscow, a three-minute drive away from the Lefortovo address, which Netto reduced to two minutes as he handled the speeding, siren-blaring ambulance.

Netto swung the ambulance to a sharp halt. Donning an orange-and-blue EMERCOM coat, Sokolov snatched his medical kit and rushed out of the vehicle. Stacie and Netto trailed him inside a building which had fallen into a dangerous state of disrepair. Sokolov charged up the stairs, stopping at the door marked *8*. He yanked the door handle, only to find it locked. He pressed the buzzer, but no reply came. He gestured to Netto.

Netto produced a set of lock picks and started working on the ancient lock.

Stacie's brows arched in surprise.

"You never told me that your friend was a burglar!" she murmured to Sokolov.

"Lock picking is a required skill for emergency responders. Sometimes people get trapped, locking themselves in by accident."

"Oh," she said, her face showing that she couldn't imagine living in such appalling conditions, let alone getting trapped inside.

"Got it," said Netto, swinging the door open.

Sokolov stepped into the brightly-lit apartment, finding himself inside a home church. He detected a blood smudge on the light switch. Another red splotch traced a path across the linoleum floor. He strode into the adjacent room, where he found his brother. Constantine was leaning in a lifeless pose on a couch, his back pressed against the wall, his neck craned sideways. Blood stains covered the jacket around a bullet hole in the arm, and another one in the torso.

Sokolov came closer and checked his pulse.

Constantine was breathing.

"Thank God you're alive."

With a pained groan, Constantine opened his eyes.

"Thank God you are, too."

Sokolov retrieved a chair from the church room, dropped his medical bag on the seat and unzipped it.

"Gene, you should introduce me to your new assistant," Constantine said as Stacie quietly entered the room. "Baroness Oltersdorf, I presume?"

"I'm Stacie," she said. "And it's Anastacia Rose, not Oltersdorf, actually."

Sokolov put on a pair of gloves and examined his brother's wounds, drawing a long breath.

"It's not as bad as I feared. The bullet that hit your arm went clean through, missing blood vessels. The wound in your side looks like nothing more than a graze. You're extremely lucky."

The bandaging was a different matter. Obviously, Constantine had dressed the wounds by himself.

Together, Sokolov and Stacie applied new dressings. Sokolov admired Stacie's composure. She never lost her calm even as she helped him stitch up the wound in Constantine's side. Her father had taught her the basics well. Sokolov didn't have to instruct her. Their efficient teamwork wasn't lost on Constantine.

"You make a fine couple."

Stacie's cheeks flushed red.

As he saw her blushing, Constantine added, "A great pair of doctors, I mean."

Sokolov injected him with a shot of antibiotics and inserted an IV drip for a saline infusion.

"There, that's better. In a week's time, you'll feel as fit as an ox. It's going to hurt for a while, but you've been shot twice, after all. Now tell me how it happened."

Constantine recounted the details of his meetings with Ilia and Orlovsky.

Apostasy. The damning word hung in the air as he explained the history of the Russian Church.

When he finished, a stunned Stacie said, "Wait a minute, let me get this straight. Are you saying that the Moscow Patriarchate is an intelligence agency?"

"Not in the conventional sense," Constantine answered. "The Soviet security apparatus shared few similarities with its Western counterparts. You see, the FSB, SVR, KGB, NKVD, all hail from the Cheka. They call themselves *Chekists* to this day, priding in their origin. From its formation in 1917, the Cheka never functioned as an intelligence service. It was the military wing of the Bolshevik Party. An instrument of Red Terror. Its name stood for Extraordinary Commission for Fighting Counter-Revolution. *Fighting*, not intelligence-gathering. Extermination. The Cheka Russian intelligence officers. Men like Peter Oltersdorf."

"The baron was a spy?" asked Stacie with even greater surprise in her voice.

"A mathematician, rather. Chief cryptographer in the Imperial Russian Army. During the First World War, he solved German and Austrian codes."

"We've recovered his notebook as well as the codebook which deciphers it," Sokolov told Constantine, and went on to update him on the Hong Kong incident.

"Are you serious? You've actually got the Oltersdorf books with you?"

"Yes," said Stacie. "Each is the size of a small diary. I have them both in my purse."

"May I have a look?" Netto chimed in.

"Sure, why not. Perhaps you might identify the code. Unless we figure out the way it works, the notebook will remain unreadable."

She placed the two leather-bound books side by side atop the desk.

As Netto carefully turned the pages of each notebook, a befuddled expression set on his face.

"I only see blocks of random, unintelligible text," Netto said. "Letters and numbers, arranged in columns."

"Like I said, we don't even know what the puzzle is, much less how to crack it."

"I do," said Constantine. "I know exactly what this is. Although I've never seen it crafted in such an elegant style."

"I'm still a bit confused," said Stacie.

"So am I," Netto added.

"This, my friends," said Constantine, "is a one-time pad."

6

"All secrets require security. When sensitive data was first put into writing, its meaning had to be concealed. Thus, cryptography began millennia ago. And so did cryptanalysis, driven by the opposite desire—to uncover hidden information. The earliest known cryptanalyst was perhaps Daniel, the Biblical prophet."

"I remember the story of Belshazzar's feast," said Stacie. "Do you mean the writing on the wall?"

"*Mene, Mene, Tekel, Upharsin,*" quoted Constantine. "King Belshazzar's magicians failed to even read God's message, let alone decode it. Only Daniel was able to interpret it. The Bible also contains several examples of Atbash, a Hebrew substitution cipher. Substitution is the most common method of encryption. Julius Caesar devised his own cipher to protect his secret messages. Peter the Great and Napoleon Bonaparte did likewise. Ciphers became more complex, but from the days of the Old Testament to the twentieth century, none were perfectly secure. Every cipher was breakable. During the First World War, the opposing sides routinely intercepted and decoded each other's radiograms. Russian codes ranked among the weakest, broken by the Austro-Hungarians in three days. After the war, however, everything changed when two Americans, Gilbert Vernam and Joseph Mauborgne, invented the one-time pad. The Vernam cipher is absolutely impossible to crack."

"Even a million years from now," Netto said, "when aliens discover our ruined planet, they'll never manage to break a one-time pad."

"For the Vernam cipher to work, the key must consist of a totally random sequence of letters. Plaintext is encrypted into ciphertext using the key material. The reverse process must be performed to recover the original message."

"So, all we need now is pencil and paper?" Stacie asked.

Constantine nodded. "You can apply the keys from the codebook to decrypt the ciphertext manually. Or you could let a computer program handle the conversion into clear text instantly."

"I won't have a chance to do that any time soon," she said.

"Not if I can help," said Netto, holding his phone.

"Really?"

"I you don't mind, I'll scan the pages with the camera. The images will sync with my workstation. As soon as I get back home, I'll OCR the pictures into readable text and run it through the crypto tool. I can get it all done today."

"Sounds fantastic."

Netto fired up the camera app and opened the notebook carefully. He snapped quick photo bursts, adjusting the phone's position for maximum quality.

"Maybe my great-grandfather will become less of a mystery for me."

"I can tell you something about him that might surprise you," said Constantine.

"I'd love to learn any details of his life."

"As the civil war broke out, he joined the White Movement. As a matter of historical record, he fought in the army of Admiral Kolchak."

"Kolchak." Stacie shook her head. "I don't think I'm familiar with the name."

"Admiral Alexander Kolchak was the acknowledged leader of all anti-communist forces in Russia. He set up a provisional Russian Government in Siberia, becoming the last legitimate head of state in this country. In 1919, his forces numbered 300,000 troops, controlling territory from the Volga River to the Pacific Ocean. However, the Bolsheviks regrouped and broke through the Ural Mountains. The Red Army advanced deep into Siberia, forcing Kolchak's troops to retreat. Losing ground, they were unable to hold off the Bolshevik hordes rolling across the vast Siberian plains. Only a few months later, Kolchak's disorganized army was defeated, and the Admiral himself was subsequently murdered by his captors. Not only did the Bolsheviks capture their sworn enemy, but they also seized the Russian gold reserve which had been evacuated eastward. Or at least, the Reds got some of it. The major portion vanished. It's been missing to date."

"Hold on, are you talking about lost treasure?"

"The entire gold fund of the Russian Empire was transported across Siberia by railroad, away from the attacking Reds. Gold bullion. Forty freight cars loaded with more than 10,000 crates of gold bars and several thousand bags of gold coins. Five to six hundred tons of gold in total. Even at the time, the exact quantity was incalculable. Not to mention another four hundred tons of silver, as well as jewelry and works of art. Kolchak had spent some of it on the war effort, procuring arms and supplies from the foreign Allies who later betrayed him. Another part fell to the Reds. The rest has never been found. Two hundred tons. Perhaps more."

"And it's real? The gold isn't just some legend?"

"It does exist. Ever since its disappearance in 1920, some have believed that the treasure was buried in a church. Whether that claim is true or not, the gold must still be hidden somewhere in Siberia."

"If you're suggesting that this is what the Chekists have been hunting for ... "

"It has to be the secret which Baron Oltersdorf was guarding with his life. I'm confident that the location of Kolchak's gold is revealed in the notebook."

Suddenly, Netto's phone rang.

"It's the Minister."

"Put him on speakerphone," said Eugene.

Klimov's voice sounded stern.

"Pavel, is Gene around?"

"I'm right here."

"Gene, I need you to report to my office immediately. We have a crisis. National security is at stake."

"I'm on my way."

"Also, that girl you've brought with you from Hong Kong."

"What about her?"

"I'd like to hear her side of the story. It's relevant to the developing situation. Is she in any condition to be present alongside you?"

Eugene gave her a questioning look, and Stacie nodded her agreement.

"We'll be there together."

"Excellent. I expect to see you both within twenty minutes."

Klimov ended the call.

Before Netto could switch to the camera app and take another picture, Stacie tucked her great-grandfather's notebooks back inside her purse.

Eugene placed a hand on Constantine's shoulder.

"Looks like we don't have much time. But I can't leave you here like this."

"Just go. Don't worry about me. You've patched me up pretty good. Nobody can find me here. It's probably the safest place in Moscow right now. I don't need babysitting."

"All right, but I promise I'll come back sooner than you think."

7

Netto, Sokolov and Stacie descended the stairs and exited the building. As Netto started toward the ambulance car, Sokolov halted him.

"Wait, Pavel. Hand me the keys."

"What? Why?"

"I want you to remain here and look after Constantine. Despite his bravado, I'd rather you kept an eye on him. Stay put until we return. Got it?"

"Okay, boss."

Netto did as he was told and gave the car keys to Sokolov. As Stacie got inside the ambulance next to him, Sokolov started the engine and the vehicle sped away.

For a few seconds Netto just stood there in the empty, dimly lit street.

Then he fetched his phone and checked his outgoing email status. The progress bar slowly crept toward completion. Mobile data speed in the area left much to be desired.

Nervously, he eyed the grim urban landscape. Lefortovo was a place that made him shudder even thinking about it. Being anywhere near Lefortovo Prison proved unbearable. He had endured a miserable few hours of solitary confinement inside the prison. In order to get out, he'd agreed to cooperate with the FSB. He'd been spying on Sokolov ever since.

A notification popped up, showing that the pictures of the Oltersdorf notebook had been sent.

He called the recipient. Anton Minski, his FSB handler. The man with the power to lock him up for good. The FSB owned the kangaroo courts that passed for the country's legal system. Through intimidation, imprisonment or direct action, the FSB had everything and everyone under their control. What was the point of acting tough like Constantine did? The FSB always got what they wanted. As far as Netto was concerned, he didn't want to get hurt in the process. Minski was a cynical, arrogant bastard who enjoyed impunity. Coming from a Chekist family, young Anton quickly rose through FSB ranks in his quest for personal profit. He didn't care about the lives he ruined. Netto knew that Minski would crush him as soon as he stopped being useful. There would be hell to pay if Netto withheld the Oltersdorf information from him. Netto now held a get-out-of-jail card and he had to play it smart.

"You'd better come up with something decent this time, Pavel," Minski spoke in a gruff voice.

"Check your inbox."

"Just what the hell is it?"

"Proof that I've managed to locate Constantine Sokolov."

"Very good. We've moved heaven and earth trying to find the bastard in this damned city."

"I could tell that by his wounds."

"How did you find him?"

"I've been asked to help with the Oltersdorf papers."

Netto could hear Minski draw a sharp breath.

"Did you say Oltersdorf?"

"Yes, and I know exactly what that means to you. Sokolov and his brother got the two notebooks. I've sent you a few sample pages."

"Give me the rest of it. I need to have everything."

"It's a bit more complicated than that. Eugene's gone somewhere and he took the notebooks with him. I've stayed behind with Constantine. He's mending a couple of bullet holes."

"Tell me where to find you. I'll take care of the rest."

"I want something in return."

"What exactly? Money?"

"Position. I want to be off the hook. I'm sick of working as a double agent and fearing for my future. A man of my talents should have a regular career at the FSB. I've shown you my worth."

"I guess you're right. You've acquitted yourself. Fear not. Once I get the Oltersdorf papers, I'm joining the league of real heavy hitters. I'll have bigger fish to fry but I could put in a word for you to my superiors. I can promise you that much."

"Do we have a deal?"

"You'll soon get your new status. Consider it done."

"Very well."

Netto spelled out the address of the safe house.

"Excellent," Minski said. "I'll send my man there. Make sure you stay out of the way. I'm a humanist. I don't want too many corpses."

"Wait, it's not supposed to be like this!"

Minski snickered. "In for a penny, in for a pound."

8

Sokolov and Stacie arrived for debriefing at the EMERCOM Headquarters on Theater Drive. Standing four stories high near the Bolshoi Theater, the former 'revenue house' carried shrapnel marks on its nineteenth-century façade—the result of a recent terrorist bombing, Sokolov explained.

On the top floor, they entered Klimov's office. The cavernous room produced an air of authority. Glossy parquet flooring of solid oak covered the entire 200-square-meter area, complemented by the darker wood of the wall panels. In full uniform, Klimov sat alone at the head of an empty conference desk that stretched before him. Two flags stood next to the entrance—the Russian flag and the EMERCOM flag, which featured an eight-pointed star on a blue background. The wall behind the general was dominated by a formidable map of the Russian Federation.

Klimov rose to greet his visitors and Sokolov made the introductions. Nikolai Klimov had a lean frame. He was even taller than Sokolov but not as muscular. His short dark hair had touches of silver at the temples. Despite their apparent difference in age and rank, the two men shook hands cordially. Their eyes showed genuine camaraderie. Klimov's gentle handshake and a warm smile put Stacie at ease. As she took her seat behind the massive desk with Sokolov, she no longer felt awed by the surroundings.

Sokolov recounted the events following his mission to Thailand and Stacie told her part of the story. Klimov listened intently, sometimes asking about specific details. The revelations of Father Mark proved to be of particular interest to him. Stacie produced the Oltersdorf notebooks to back up their report. When they finished, Klimov let out a pensive sigh.

"It confirms my own findings. I was hoping I got this one wrong, but you've left me no room for doubt."

"What happened while I was away?" Sokolov asked.

"It's not about what *did* happen, but rather what *didn't*. At nine a.m. today, a scheduled event we were supposed to monitor never occurred. We expected increased seismic activity in a certain part of eastern Siberia. Yet our Seismological Data Center issued no alerts. At the designated hour, it registered nothing."

"You don't mean ..." Sokolov paused. "That would be unthinkable."

A shadow crossed Klimov's face.

"Gene, you know that I hate politics. As a minister in the federal government, I've seen my share of power plays. I'm no saint. Sometimes I'm dragged into things that leave a nasty taste in my mouth. I've turned a blind eye on a few false-flag operations in the past, convincing myself that I was choosing the lesser of two evils. But a line must be drawn somewhere. I don't want to end up like Shoigu, the founder of our agency. I can't go against my conscience and sit around idly as a terrorist plot is unfolding before my eyes."

"I'm sorry but what's going on?" asked Stacie, confused.

"A nuclear explosive device has gone missing in Siberia," said Klimov. "I believe it's the final piece of Operation Temple as you described it."

Stacie stared in astonishment. "How is it even possible to steal a nuclear bomb?"

"Have you heard of PNEs?"

Stacie shook her head.

"Peaceful nuclear explosions," Sokolov explained.

"I've no idea what that means."

"Like my brother is fond of saying, the Soviet Union was only capable of destruction, not creation. Communism stifled all original thought. You'd imagine that the invention of the atomic bomb required some creative genius, but it was impossible in an impoverished, war-torn country under Stalin's rule. Igor Kurchatov is recognized as the father of the Soviet nuclear program, but he was clueless about physics. Kurchatov was a Chekist, not a researcher. An NKVD man tasked by Beria with overseeing the project. The real father of the bomb was German physicist Manfred von Ardenne, taken to the USSR together with hundreds of other ex-Nazi scientists and their equipment in 1945. Once the German secrets fell into their hands, the Soviets became a nuclear superpower. They wanted to show it off in the Cold

War race for ideological supremacy, but the military side had to remain classified. So they came up with a civil use for atomic weapons. They called it Program 7, coining the term *Nuclear Explosions for the National Economy*."

"The crazy experiments performed under Program 7 were nothing short of criminal," Klimov commented.

"The most striking example came during 1965 with the *Chagan* detonation, when the Soviets violated a test ban treaty in Kazakhstan. A 140-kiloton bomb produced a giant crater which dammed the Chagan River and formed a water reservoir. Thus it became the first man-made radioactive lake. The fallout from the blast traveled as far as Japan."

Klimov pressed a console button and the map of Russia behind him lit up like a Christmas tree with a myriad of blinking markers. Nuclear explosion sites dotted the entire country.

"That was just a single one of at least 128 known nuclear explosions performed around the USSR over several decades."

A text overlay appeared on the map, listing each PNE:

... *1971*: **Sapphire**, 15 kilotons...

... *1972*: **Region-4**, 6.6 kilotons...

... *1978*: **Kraton-1**, 22 kilotons; **Kraton-2**, 15 kilotons; **Kraton-3**, 22 kilotons...

... *1982*: **Rift-1**, 16 kilotons...

... *1984*: **Quarz-4**, 10 kilotons...

The list went on and on.

"My God," Stacie said as her eyes scanned it.

Klimov continued. "The intended application of PNEs involved earth-moving, ore-crushing, stimulation of oil production, or geological exploration. In most cases, the use of nuclear devices proved completely unwarranted and resulted in radioactive pollution. A large number of blasts were carried out merely to study the spread of radiation. A two-kiloton PNE code-named *Globus-1* polluted a densely-populated area of the Volga in 1971. Lake Baikal, the nature's largest fresh water reserve, was contaminated following detonations between 1953 and 1982. Such catastrophes are comparable to Chernobyl or the tragedy of the Aral Sea."

"A hundredfold Chernobyl," Stacie murmured in horror.

"Program 7 shut down in 1988 as the Soviet Union neared collapse. Recently, however, it has been revived. A gas gusher is raging in Yakutia, and a decision was made to extinguish it with a PNE as the only alternative. According to EMERCOM's seismic data, it didn't go successfully. As things stand, a twenty-kiloton nuclear device remains unaccounted for. Beyond that, it's impossible to verify any information. The FSB has sealed off all access to the area. I've voiced my concerns over the possible loss of a nuclear bomb to the Kremlin and the FSB. The Kremlin is keeping silence. In a thinly veiled threat, the FSB advised me to avoid making rash accusations. They must be preparing a cover-up. The company operating the gas well has strong connections with both the FSB and the Patriarchate. It all adds up."

"So what are we going to do about it?" said Sokolov.

"First and foremost, we must bring Anastacia back to Australia safely. Stacie, you're a brave young woman, but you must realize that your life is in peril. The people we're up against will stop at nothing. With every passing minute, staying in Russia is becoming increasingly more dangerous for you. I've already arranged for an EMERCOM plane to fly you to San Francisco. Once there, you'll head over to the Australian Consulate, claim a lost passport, and return to Sydney."

She shook her head as the finality of Klimov's words sank in. Her fingers brushed over the leather-bound covers of the Oltersdorf books resting atop the conference table.

"Promise me that the secrets within these pages won't fall into the wrong hands," she said.

"They belong to you," Sokolov said. "The notebooks *and* their secrets. Don't you want to keep them?"

"But what if they really contain the whereabouts of Kolchak's gold?"

"That's beside the point, Stacie. The importance of these papers has nothing to do with lost treasures. The Oltersdorf notebooks are memories of your family's past. Your great-grandfather and your aunt left them for *you*, not someone else. Nothing else matters. You decide."

She felt a tear rolling down her cheek.

"Thank you, Eugene. I never expected to hear such words. And yet, Russia is where Baron Oltersdorf's legacy belongs. This is my decision. I want your brother to keep the papers. He deserves it as a historian and as a person." She squeezed the golden pendant on her neck. "I have enough to remind me of my family history. I hope the notebooks will remind you of me."

Sokolov nodded.

"I'll always remember you, Stacie. You can count on that. And I'll deliver the notebooks to Constantine."

"I guess it's the last goodbye, then," she said. "Thank you for everything."

"We'll meet again someday," he assured her.

Klimov broke an uneasy silence.

"Gene, speaking of your brother, you should transfer Constantine to an EMERCOM hospital right away. No time left until your next mission."

"What do you want me to do?"

"We're facing a cataclysm of global magnitude. A missing twenty-kiloton explosive device puts us on the brink of a nuclear war. If what you've told me is true, we cannot allow the North Koreans to blow up the Middle East. As an backup alternative, they might set it off somewhere in Russia. But what if they're targeting the United States? Whoever has stolen the bomb, and whatever their real plan is, it can only end in a nightmare scenario. I want you to stop them, Gene. You must find the nuclear bomb before it's too late."

9

His Holiness Patriarch Galaktion of Moscow and All Rus', Primate of the Russian Orthodox Church, did not believe in God.

The religious leader of millions of Christians never opened the Holy Scripture.

His faith was militant atheism. The only icon he'd ever worshipped was a portrait of Lenin. His sacred text was a bank ledger.

His father, Valdemar, had ended an undercover KGB career in the rank of Archbishop of the Moscow Patriarchate. Continuing the family tradition, Galaktion (secular name Anatoly Vasiliev) had reached even greater heights, becoming the Patriarch.

Galaktion wore an everyday black cassock, a white cowl covering his head, and a green cope embroidered with gold thread and jeweled like his crosier. His private collection numbered around ten thousand vestments worth a total of several million U.S. dollars, a trifle which he could well afford, having amassed a fortune to rival Russia's wealthiest oligarchs. The diamond-covered Hublot timepiece on his wrist had cost a million alone.

The Patriarch's official residence occupied a mansion built in 1816 by a famous Moscow family. Located just off Prechistenka, a few blocks away from the Cathedral of Christ the Savior, it had been 'nationalized' by the Bolsheviks following the Revolution and given to the Embassy of Germany. In 1941, the German ambassador to the USSR had been evicted from the mansion. Two years later, Stalin handed it over to his newly-formed Moscow Patriarchate. Today, an FSO security detail protected it around the clock.

Inside the mansion, Patriarch Galaktion was holding a tête-à-tête meeting in the Red Room. True to its name, the vast chamber featured maroon-colored walls and mahogany furniture.

The air smelled of fresh white roses, its stillness accentuated by a grandfather clock with each metronomic swing of its pendulum. Honorary awards from the Kremlin and the FSB lined the wall next to a life-size, oil-on-canvas portrait of Galaktion in a gilded frame.

In a wheezing voice, Galaktion spoke to his guest sitting across the table.

"What tidings do you bring, Saveliy Ignatievich?"

Frolov grinned slyly. "Your Holiness, you will be most pleased."

"Business hasn't gone too well lately. Even the vodka sales are dropping. I need something to brighten my mood."

"Operation Temple is well under way. Phase Two has begun."

Pensively, Galaktion stroked his thick, gray beard. He still had reservations about the plan. The risk seemed too great—but so was the reward. As Galaktion's long-time KGB handler, Frolov knew which buttons to push. The Patriarch preferred to play it safe, but Frolov had convinced him that they had more to lose unless they turned the tables in the great geopolitical game.

"Is everything running on schedule?"

"It couldn't have gone any better. Zeldin and his team have been eliminated. The device is currently aboard the train. As soon as it reaches North Korea, it will be shipped by sea to commence the final phase. Operation Temple is unstoppable."

"And the Oltersdorf papers?"

"Minski just got word from his snitch. After all these years, the Oltersdorf notebooks are finally here in Moscow."

Galaktion's eyes narrowed to slits.

"Any news about the girl and those who helped her?"

"I assure you that they no longer pose any threat."

"They deserve punishment."

"Don't worry, I've already sent my man to deal with them."

"Deal with them? I want them eliminated," said the Patriarch of the Lubyanka.

Frolov chuckled. "They don't have a prayer."

10

A Hyundai sedan pulled up in front of the shabby apartment block, the headlights turned off. The driver killed the engine and got out, shutting the door softly. Observing from across the street, Netto failed to make out the man's features in the dim lighting. He was of medium height and build, but there was no mistaking the purposeful stride. He was a predator prowling his hunting ground. As the man entered the building, Netto's gut feeling told him that it was the killer sent over by Minski.

His chest tightened with swelling panic. Fear mixed with guilt. He knew that he was responsible for signing Constantine's death warrant. Sokolov would realize that Netto was a mole. No one else could have tipped off the FSB. It would all end badly, Netto told himself. What if Minski had decided to get rid of him, too? Trying to bargain with Minski now seemed like a really stupid idea. Dread filled Netto at the prospect of becoming either the fall guy or someone who knew too much.

With numb fingers, he dialed Sokolov.

The endless ring-back tone was driving him mad.

Come on! Pick up the damned phone!

He cursed his luck. Sokolov was probably still in a meeting with Klimov.

The call switched to voicemail. Netto severed the connection and redialed.

At length, Sokolov answered. "I'm heading back, Pavel. What have you got?"

"Gene... Hurry. I think the safe house has been compromised."

11

Gun drawn, Victor kicked the door in and entered the apartment, searching for targets. His sights found an injured man reclining on a couch, hooked to an IV drip. The wounds were bandaged where Victor's quick shots had hit him. The bastard had been fortunate enough to remain alive but his luck had run out. With the prey finally trapped, Victor wanted to enjoy the moment to its fullest.

"We meet again, Constantine," he said. "But this time, you can't escape your death."

Instead of betraying terror or despair, Constantine Sokolov's eyes showed disdain.

"Death doesn't scare me. But I'd hate to give you the satisfaction, Comrade ... what was it? Sorry, I never bothered to remember the name of Frolov's lapdog. You're all bark but no bite, though."

Victor had never expected the bastard to mock him. He seethed.

"Is that so? That old fool Ilia thought differently before he died. He spilled his guts, and so will you. You'll tell me where the notebooks are."

Victor kicked him in the stomach, grabbed hold of his shirt and hauled him off the couch. The IV stand toppled, ripping the tube free of the catheter. Victor dragged Constantine across the floor, smashing the gun handle against his skull repeatedly. Next, he retrieved a zip-tie from his jacket pocket and locked Constantine's wrists behind his back, fastening it around the pipe of an old cast-iron radiator in the corner of the room.

Blood trickling down his neck, Constantine gritted his teeth. Those stormy gray eyes flashed with cold rage, but again showed no sign of fear. Anyone else would've already begged for mercy. Not this son of a bitch.

Victor started losing his temper. *Let's see how tough you really are.*

Lacking any suitable tools, Victor had to improvise. He barged into the adjacent kitchenette and flicked on the light switch. A cockroach scampered behind the cupboard. Victor opened the drawers, which were barren save for an empty plastic bag and a can of bug spray. He would have to make do. He slapped his handgun back into the shoulder holster and took both.

Then he opened the gas oven and twisted the knob. When he was finished, all evidence would be destroyed by the explosion resulting from the gas leak. Just another fatal accident.

He emptied the can of insecticide into the plastic bag and returned to his captive. Approaching from behind, he pulled the bag over Constantine's head and secured it tightly with another zip-tie. Constantine struggled helplessly. The exertion always made matters worse for the victim, who used up the air quicker. True enough, Constantine was suffocating within seconds, the plastic bag clinging to his face as he squirmed. With every agonizing breath, he inhaled the insecticide.

Victor picked up a wooden chair and smashed it against the floor, snapping off a leg. He swung it like a baton, raining blows on the arms and torso, hitting hard. The sudden onslaught of pain made Constantine's breathing even more rapid. The plastic smothered his anguished cries, cutting off the air supply.

Victor battered him with the chair leg until Constantine's body went limp.

12

The EMERCOM Minister's executive Mercedes-Benz raced through the streets as Sokolov hit the accelerator. Engine growling, he blitzed every pocket of space in the Moscow traffic. Beyond the Lubyanka, the heavy black sedan spurted across the Garden Ring. He beat a two-kilometer stretch, darting between lanes, cutting in front of motorists who blared their horns angrily. Turning the wheel sharply, he ignored a red traffic light as he charged toward the Third Ring Road highway. Speeding recklessly, he knew that the police would never dare confront the authority of the car's government plates.

The speedometer broke the 130 km/h mark. In a dizzying rush, the Mercedes shot along the highway, breezing past the steady flow of cars as if they were crawling. A drop in concentration would send him crashing into another vehicle. As an SUV popped up ahead of him, he braked with ice-cold precision and maneuvered away from danger, flooring the gas pedal again.

He dropped speed, navigating his way around the Lefortovo district. Sokolov glanced at his Breitling. He'd clocked under five minutes. The route normally took twenty.

The record would mean nothing if he was already too late.

He stopped the Mercedes in front of the apartment block where he'd last seen his brother. Pavel's urgent plea had provided no details, and he'd failed to get in touch with him since. Sokolov's mind painted the worst-case outcome. He had to act on the assumption that the safe house had been hit, with Constantine and Pavel either captured or killed.

From the glove box, Sokolov grabbed a Makarov PM pistol and checked the magazine. It was full, holding eight rounds. That would do.

He was short on firepower, but his best weapon remained the element of surprise.

13

In the Soviet Army, a torture method known as 'the elephant' involved placing a gas mask on the victim and blocking the flow of oxygen. A simpler asphyxiation technique with the use of a plastic bag was called 'the supermarket'. Both interrogation practices had become widespread in the Russian military and law enforcement.

Knowing this, Constantine had braced himself, but nothing could have prepared him for the torment he endured.

He clenched his jaw, biting at the plastic, trying to rip the bag with his teeth. His futile efforts became increasingly difficult. Crushing agony erupted in his lungs. Each strike against his body exploded in his oxygen-deprived brain. The poisonous chemicals burned his face and throat.

The suffering seemed endless. His limbs numbed. His mind was slipping into the abyss. As he was about to black out, Victor yanked the plastic bag off his head. Tears streamed from his bloodshot eyes as he gasped for breath. His vision blurry, he could hardly see his tormentor, but he heard his voice.

"You might think otherwise, but I'm not a sadist. I don't do it for pleasure alone. It's my duty. It's what holds our country together. Squashing insects like you. Because that's what you are. Did you enjoy a taste of insecticide?" Victor laughed. "You're too bold. Judging by your reaction, I bet it's Eugene who has the notebooks. Perhaps we'll have to wait until he comes back. He wouldn't leave his wounded brother alone to die here, would he? Then again, I don't have that much time on my hands. It's easier to kill you one by one. You, your brother, and that girl. I'll have some fun with her, too."

Victor flipped the chair leg in his hand.

"But first, I'll give you one last chance before I kill you. Unless you talk, I'll put the bag back on while I sodomize you with the chair leg. I wish I could rape your girlfriend as well. I do remember her name. Nina, right?"

Constantine's rage burst out in a guttural roar.

"Don't you dare mention her name, you piece of filth."

The words came from Eugene, who was aiming a gun at the assassin's head.

14

The killer pivoted to face Sokolov.

"Don't shoot!" he said, holding his hands up defensively.

Sokolov had realized what was going on even before he'd crossed the apartment's threshold. The screams sounding from within had made his blood boil. He'd stormed inside to discover the killer standing over Constantine.

Sokolov saw that his brother had been severely beaten. Tied to a radiator, he lay unmoving on the floor, his face red from asphyxiation, scalp bleeding.

Locking the assailant in the sights of the Makarov pistol, Sokolov recognized the man's average-looking features.

"Drop your weapons and step away from him!" Sokolov commanded.

Victor tossed aside the broken chair leg. Then, careful to use only his thumb and forefinger, he extracted the gun from his holster and let it fall. Moving away from Constantine, Victor kicked the kitchenette door open.

"Do you smell that odor in the air?" Victor said. "It's a gas leak. The muzzle flash from the Makarov or a ricochet could be enough to ignite it. Are you willing to risk your life and cause an explosion? You'd kill your brother, too. Hell, the whole building would go up. And you care so much about other people's lives, don't you? It only takes a spark. You should know that, rescue boy."

"Only with the right gas-to-air ratio."

"You sure if it's within the limits? Well, go ahead and take a gamble. Pull the trigger. Blow up the whole damned place. Or put that gun away and take me on. Fight like a man, Eugene."

Sokolov threw a glance in the direction of the gas oven. Natural gas was colorless and odorless, but for domestic use, an odorant was added to it so that consumers could easily detect a leak. Ethyl mercaptan in this case, which stank of rotten cabbage. Sokolov felt the pungent scent drifting into the room.

If it was a ploy, it had worked. Sokolov hesitated with his shot as Victor suddenly dashed at him.

Contrary to popular belief, Spetsnaz troops received almost no training in hand-to-hand combat. Their main skills included running and gunning. The last thing on the mind of any Russian soldier was engaging in a punch-out. An ex-GRU assassin would never leave himself unarmed.

Sokolov saw the flash of a blade. Victor attacked with a knife.

Sokolov tried to fend off the oncoming blow, but it knocked out the Makarov from his grip. The pistol clattered, sliding across the floor. Blood drops spattered the linoleum. Sokolov's hand was bleeding where Victor had nicked it.

Before Victor managed to swipe again, Sokolov pushed him away with a *mae geri* front kick to the abdomen and retreated quickly. Searing pain shot through his cut hand.

Victor was brandishing a 'Finnish' knife utilized by the NKVD since the 1940s, so called because it had been fashioned after the traditional *puukko* knife of Finnish huntsmen. The modern NR-40 version featured an S-shaped guard and a large clip point. Longer than a true *puukko*, the 150-mm blade had a curving cutting edge and a flat back. For a brief moment, Sokolov regretted not carrying his dive knife. Victor had all the initiative. Real-life knife fights resembled ugly, furious slaughter instead of fencing duels. Once within range, the killer would carve him up. He could slice muscles and tendons, and wait for Sokolov to bleed out, or stab vital organs to finish him in a matter of seconds. Sokolov had nothing to defend himself with against a deadly weapon. Fighting barehanded, he wouldn't last long, despite his karate expertise. The trickle of blood running down his arm manifested his slim odds.

Timing and movement were key. Sokolov quelled his fear. He kept an eye on the *puukko*, knowing that all attempts to hold off the attacker were destined to fail. He entertained no fantasies about disarming his opponent. Waiting for the perfect moment to catch the knife arm spelled suicide. A single cut was enough to inflict lethal damage. Sokolov was determined to destroy him first. He had to take Victor out with brutal force and sharp reflexes, leaving no chance of retaliation. It meant coming out on top in a split-second clash.

Sokolov sidestepped, closing in laterally. Superior footwork improved his offensive and defensive angles, and he needed every advantage he could gain.

Victor feinted, throwing out his empty hand to create an opening for a follow-up lethal blow. Keeping the knife-hand retracted close to his body, he swung his left fist at Sokolov. Then he lunged forward, thrusting the blade in a lightning-quick blur.

Survival or death.

The knife attack came in fast and hard—a violent, prison-style stabbing.

An instant before the knife thrust was able to gut him, Sokolov shattered Victor's jaw with a savage punch. He'd struck faster and harder.

The killer toppled. The *puukko* slipped from his fingers as he tumbled to the floor like a sack of bricks.

Sokolov made sure he stayed down. He pinned Victor to the ground. He had to finish the job. Only one of them would remain alive—whoever seized hold of the knife first.

As Victor grasped for the knife handle next to him, Sokolov snatched it from his reach. In one swift motion, Sokolov dragged the blade against Victor's neck, slitting his throat.

The assassin's eyes bulged in horror as blood geysered from the severed carotid artery. With his windpipe cut open, he gulped for air in mute protest, but he was paying the price for attempting to murder Sokolov. A kill-or-be-killed encounter demanded ruthlessness.

Then Victor lost consciousness, his brain shutting down without a blood supply.

Sokolov pushed himself away from his incapacitated enemy.

Victor would die in a couple of minutes, but Sokolov wasn't quite out of the woods yet.

His heart thudded. He turned to his brother. Constantine lay completely still, eyes shut.

Sokolov's own breathing was becoming labored, signaling a dangerous level of gas concentration. In a few more minutes, dizziness would set in. After passing out, they would both die.

Still holding the gore-splattered knife, he picked himself off the floor and staggered toward the oven. He gagged as he switched the gas off. Returning to the room, he unlatched every window and swung it wide open. Fresh air coursed inside.

Sokolov bent down to snip off the zip-tie locking his brother's hands to the radiator.

"Can you move? You need to get up."

"I'll try ... " Constantine squinted. "My whole body hurts like hell."

"We need to get out of here as soon as possible."

In haste, Sokolov picked up the PM handgun and wrapped a bandage over his wounded hand, grabbing an unused gauze roll left on the table. Then he propped Constantine up, slipping an arm under his shoulder. Constantine winced in pain, shuffling his feet as Sokolov helped him outside.

They descended the two flights of steps, made it out into the dark street and approached the Mercedes, activating its keyless entry and engine start-up. Constantine got in the back while Sokolov jumped in the driving seat. The heavy sedan accelerated. The safe house receded in the rearview mirror. The death scene inside it was etched vividly on Sokolov's mind. He couldn't believe they had escaped the nightmare.

"We're safe," he told Constantine. "Just hang in there, we'll make it to the hospital in no time."

"I feel like I've been run over by a truck. I got badly bruised, a few broken bones maybe, but it could've been much worse. He was only getting started when you came to the rescue. I should be alright soon."

The mental scars would be harder to heal, Sokolov didn't say.

"What about Stacie? Is she okay?" Constantine asked.

"She's under protection, on her way back home. The Oltersdorf books are locked in a vault inside Klimov's office. Stacie will be out of danger on Australian soil. She can lead a normal life now."

"Thank God. And Pavel? Where is he?"

"Wasn't he there when the killer showed up?"

"No. In fact, he never came back after you left together."

"Yeah, I'd like to know the answer," Sokolov said with steel in his voice. "Just where the hell has he been?"

15

While Eugene accompanied Constantine in intensive care, a white EMERCOM van pulled up at the death scene they had left an hour earlier. Sergei Zubov got out from driver's seat and opened the rear door to retrieve his gear. He pulled out a gurney and adjusted its collapsible undercarriage to the fully-extended position. Fetching two equipment bags made from heavy-duty tarpaulin, he stacked them on top of the gurney and wheeled it inside the building. Reaching the second-floor apartment, he unlocked the front door with the key he'd taken from Sokolov, rolled the gurney in, and closed the door behind him.

In the narrow hallway, Zubov unzipped the bag which contained his protective clothing. He donned a head-to-toe hazmat suit, rubber overboots, a pair of gloves, and a respirator mask. Decontamination of the scene from human remains and bodily fluids required adequate biohazard protection.

Zubov had seen plenty of dead bodies in disaster areas, so he had the stomach for it. Not that it made the experience any less gruesome. As he discovered the corpse, Zubov realized that he had his work cut out for him. The assassin had died a messy death. Blood covered the floor all around the body. Zubov laid out a cadaver pouch, placed the body inside and sealed it. Working on his own, it took more effort than he'd expected. Beads of sweat rolled down his forehead. The hazmat suit felt uncomfortable, trapping Zubov's body heat.

He mopped up the blood spills off the linoleum using a compact-yet-powerful wet vacuum cleaner. The potential items of evidence were consigned to a biohazard waste bag: the assassin's handgun, the zip-ties, the IV bag, syringes, and other medical supplies left by Sokolov. The hardest part came next. Meticulously, he wiped every surface with a hospital-grade disinfectant to get rid of blood smudges and fingerprints. The arduous task took hours to complete. Zubov doubled his efforts, battling against time. He had a strict schedule to keep. Utterly exhausted by the time he finished, Zubov stripped off the hazmat outfit and trashed it into another waste bag. Then, he lowered the gurney, hauled the cadaver pouch onto it, and secured the straps. He packed the cleaning tools and placed the equipment bags on the gurney's bottom frame. As he trundled the gurney outside, he wished he had some assistance, but Sokolov had told him that he could trust nobody outside their team.

Unfolding the van's access ramp, he transferred the gurney back inside the vehicle. All kinds of lowlifes loitered about the streets at night, but so far the neighborhood had seemed deserted. As he climbed into the driver's seat, he was pretty sure he'd managed to avoid detection.

By daybreak, he was long gone.

He drove the van outside the city limits. Turning off the highway, he took a rural road. After a rough few kilometers, he reached a barren, secluded area of former farmland.

Zubov rapped his fingers on the steering wheel as he eyed the dashboard clock.

Ten minutes later, an enormous Volvo truck appeared in view, parking next to Zubov's van.

The truck was pulling an intermodal container. It looked like a standard twenty-foot model, except for a chimney pipe extending from the middle of the roof.

Zubov's partner, Mischenko, climbed out of the Volvo. A hulking bear of a man with a bearded, Slavic face, Mischenko opened the container doors.

The shipping container housed an incinerator.

The Russian-built mobile incineration unit was designed for medical waste disposal or the cremation of fallen livestock. It cremated horse, cattle, and pig carcasses at a rate of forty kilograms per hour. Diesel-fueled, the incinerator weighed seven tons and heated to a combustion temperature of 850-1200 degrees Celsius, burning 97 percent of the waste volume. Mischenko had 'borrowed' it from an EMERCOM disease prevention facility outside Moscow.

Rumors claimed that similar incinerators had been employed to cover up military actions in Ukraine, destroying the bodies of slain soldiers. Zubov and Mischenko prepared to put that theory to the test.

Mischenko pressed a button on the control panel to start a burn cycle. It reached the minimum required temperature in twenty minutes.

Together, Zubov and Mischenko opened the access lid and loaded the cadaver pouch off the gurney into the furnace chamber.

At such high temperatures, the incinerator produced no black smoke, emitting an environmentally-friendly gas mixture.

Two hours later, all that remained of the assassin was a handful of ash inside the incinerator's afterburner.

16

The punch sent Netto reeling as Sokolov slugged him across the face.

"I swear I'm not a mole!"

"You're no mole, all right. You're a rat."

Blood oozed from Netto's split lower lip.

Sokolov had cornered him in his hacker's den—the cluttered apartment where Netto ate and slept when he wasn't working on his Linux rig.

"I'm sorry, okay? What I did was wrong. I ran off because I got scared!"

"*Cowards die many times before their deaths*, Pavel. And traitors are the worst kind of cowards. They live in constant fear."

"You got it all wrong, Gene. If I tipped the FSB off, then why would I warn you about the killer? Come on, it doesn't make sense."

"You set me up. You wanted to get me and my brother both killed. Cut the act, Judas. You're lucky I'm the one who came knocking on your door this morning. When your Chekist friends figure out that their assassin is dead, heads will roll. And first of all, it'll be *your* head—literally. Your limbs and torso will be dumped somewhere else."

Netto blanched. Denying his treachery became pointless.

"Dear God ... What am I going to do?" he mumbled.

"For starters, tell me how you got mixed up with them. While you're at it, get down to work. To save your skin, you must recover all of the data from this tablet."

Sokolov handed him the device he'd taken off Song.

Netto whimpered. "Your wish is my command. Please, don't hurt me. I swear I can acquit myself."

"We'll see about that."

Netto connected the tablet to his workstation and hit the keyboard, typing commands in a terminal window.

"They snatched me as I was walking home," he began, detailing his horrific experience inside Lefortovo Prison.

As Sokolov listened to the story, his contempt for FSB tactics reached a new level. But although he could rationalize the motives of Netto's betrayal, Sokolov would never be able to forgive his former friend.

"There. I retrieved your guy's Darkmail credentials. Seems like he deleted his email conversations regularly, but there are several messages in the trash which he failed to wipe out. I've restored them. The sent mail is written in Korean, but there's one incoming message he received from Minski. It says: *Everything's OK. The merchandise will ship on schedule.*"

"Are you sure it's from him? I don't see his name."

"I've been sending weekly reports to this very address. Minski keeps me on a short leash. I couldn't even pack my bags and run—he'd find me anywhere. You don't know what a bastard he is."

"I do," Sokolov said. "He's a hoodlum blinded by greed. His ambition to climb to the top of the Chekist hierarchy makes him bite off more than he can chew. And I got the perfect bait for him. Or rather, he thinks that *you* have it. And you'll give it to him."

"What do you mean?"

"He's desperate to pull off a coup. He won't be able to resist the Oltersdorf secrets. Why don't you yank his chain?"

"How?"

"You'll send him an email. Instead of the Oltersdorf pages, it will contain a virus. I want you to hack into his computer and plunder the entire contents of the hard drive. Then you'll need to find a needle in a haystack."

"Such as?"

"Any mention of Operation Temple. Especially, anything in regard to transportation. The railroad is the most secure and reliable link between Russia and the North Korea. The Kremlin has invested heavily to revamp the North Korean railway system. I want to know which train they're using for cargo delivery. Is it doable?"

Netto shrugged. "Why the hell not. It's not the Bushehr Nuclear Power Plant in Iran that you're asking me to penetrate."

"I wouldn't take no for an answer. But what if you're targeting the wrong machine?"

"I can find a backdoor to the entire government server if necessary. I'll use Minski's system to infiltrate his contacts and keep looking until I hit the right result. Most of the FSB officials I've met are complacent idiots when it comes to network security. They don't believe that a classified data leak could happen to them in their own backyard. Yeah, I'll do it, Gene. I can write the required malware. As things stand, I'm finished. But if I steal some of Minski's secrets, maybe I'll have the insurance I need against him."

The FSB had welcomed scum like Snowden with open arms. The irony of putting them on the receiving end of a cyberattack wasn't lost on Sokolov.

"Get started."

"I'm on it. Whether it turns out to be a train, an airplane, or a dog sled crossing into North Korea, I promise I'll pinpoint it for you."

Netto spent the better part of the next hour hammering the keys as he tweaked the Trojan source code.

"When he opens this message, the worm will give me full access to his desktop. It can replicate and spread around his network, infecting hundreds of other PCs." Netto launched a Windows virtual machine and showed Sokolov how the malicious code worked step by step. "All right, it's your call. I'm one keystroke away from sending the email."

"Do it."

Emphatically, Netto jabbed the Enter key with his index finger.

The response came a few anxious seconds later.

Upon reading the message, Minski had opened the attachment immediately.

Lines of code ran across the screen.

"Hook, line, and sinker," Netto said. "I'm scanning his drives right now."

The worm had been running for thirty minutes when Netto let out a low whistle.

"Jackpot."

"You found something?"

"Oh yeah! I hit pay dirt in one of his hidden folders. A huge collection of gay porn, including some potentially scandalous stuff with Minski himself."

"Don't try my patience while I'm still being nice to you."

Once a snake, always a snake, thought Sokolov. No matter how much he despised Minski, he'd never stoop to dirty-laundry blackmail. Netto, on the other hand, had no qualms about using the FSB man's own methods against him. Sokolov wondered how eager Netto had been to stab him in the back on Minski's demand. The two of them were of the same ilk. Sokolov decided that soiling his hands to teach Netto a lesson wasn't even worth it. As punishment, he'd let the snitch and the handler fight it out between themselves, going at each other's throats.

Sokolov kept a close eye on the computer monitor, making sure he never gave Netto another chance to double-cross him.

Netto selected multiple files from the growing list of search results.

"And ... here it is. A few hundred pages' worth of technical documentation."

Several windows popped up on the display as Netto opened the PDF files side by side. He scrolled through the pages quickly.

Three documents in particular caught Sokolov's attention.

The first file provided a full description of the nuclear explosive device.

Next came the specifications of a Soviet-built M62 diesel-electric locomotive.

The last document listed the itinerary of a 56-car freight train traveling to the North Korean sea port of Rason.

17

Through the helicopter window, Sokolov studied the rugged terrain first discovered by his ancestors.

In the 1580s, an 800-man-strong Cossack force had conquered the Siberian Kingdom, presenting it to the Moscow Czar as a gift. The Cossack explorers had endowed Russia with a land of riches. For centuries to come, Siberia would provide a source of limitless wealth, from gold, silver, gemstones and sable, to crude oil and natural gas.

No other empire had expanded as peacefully as Russia under the rule of the benevolent Christian czars. Siberia had seen the rise of the Russian Empire and its fall.

Alexander Kolchak, Russia's last legitimate ruler, had been murdered in Siberia, his dead body dumped under the ice of the Angara River flowing from Lake Baikal. The last Czar, Nicholas II and his family had endured captivity in the Siberian town of Tobolsk before their slaughter.

Sokolov remembered the argument he'd had with his brother.

"*Everyone betrayed the Czar,*" Constantine had said. "*The generals, the aides, the Russian elite. They all watched idly as the Imperial Family was killed. Everyone, including the Russian people. They'd done nothing to protect their monarch from the massacre. And by the time the killing reached their own families, it was already too late. Unless the Russian nation repents of the horrifying regicide allowed by their forefathers, this country will remain cursed forever.*"

"*Fair enough. The blood of the Romanovs is on their hands. But unlike Nicholas II, the previous Emperors had known how to deal with their own entourage. The generals who betrayed him were the ones he'd handpicked. He had only himself to blame. He failed as a leader. He was the anointed sovereign, and yet he abdicated. Instead of having the traitors hanged, he'd chosen to become their victim. In the country's darkest hour, how could he surrender the monarch's duty? He doomed himself and he doomed Russia."*

The beheaded country had plunged into civil war. Siberia had bled. No other part of Russia had suffered such annihilation. A hellish carnival of death had swept across the Siberian plains, reaping human lives by the millions. Ravaging Siberia through war, mass murder, and epidemic typhus, the Bolsheviks had drowned the once-prosperous land in blood. And from that slush of gore and lice, they'd raised the archipelago—nay, a continent—of the Gulag.

Trains had linked the gulag system together, allowing it to function, transferring millions of people to the communist prison camps. The railroads had become subsidiary to the gulags. Unsurprisingly, the director of the Cheka, Felix Dzerzhinsky, had also headed the Soviet Transport Commissariat, a position subsequently taken by Lazar Kaganovich, Stalin's chief henchman.

The entire Soviet economy had relied on slave labor, with the victims fortifying the rule of their oppressors. Under communism, the mind-boggling construction projects had doubled as death camps. The workers had fallen dead building factories, power plants and railroads, with new waves of inmates just like themselves laying bricks and rails over their frozen bones before perishing as well. The Bolsheviks had wasted human life in pursuit of their goals which, once reached, they had found useless, such as the Baikal-Amur Mainline. A new railway network running parallel to the Trans-Siberian Railway, it had failed to serve any practical purpose beyond its six-figure death toll. Intended as a show of Bolshevik superiority, it had remained unfinished for seven decades, losing in every respect to the Trans-Siberian Railway built under the Czar whom the Bolsheviks had killed.

Stretching over 5,000 miles, completed from 1891 to 1916, the great Trans-Siberian Railway still acted as the main travel route across Eurasia. It had a maximum transit capacity of 120 million tons of cargo per year, and dozens of freight trains coursed it daily.

But on the designated day of the nuclear blast, there had been only one train running to North Korea. Number 4001.

Trans-Siberian trains traveled at an average of 30 km/h, hitting top speeds of 50 km/h. According to Sokolov's calculations, no other train could have picked up the nuclear device, which had likely been delivered from the blowout site by aircraft. The timing of the heist had been planned to perfection. He'd also noticed that thirteen passenger trains had been delayed for up to seventeen hours, the timetables adjusted to create a safety buffer around No. 4001, giving it a clear path all the way to the Khasan-Rason border link.

Sokolov didn't believe in coincidences, but educated guesswork could only get him so far. A recon flyover would determine whether he was right. He was inside an EMERCOM Kamov Ka-32A11BC search-and-rescue chopper, trying to locate and identify the North Korean train. Originally designed for Arctic anti-submarine warfare, the Kamov boasted great maneuverability thanks to its coaxial rotors. A thermoelectric de-icing system made it ideal for operating in Siberian conditions.

The railroad snaked through the frozen Siberian tundra. It was forsaken territory. Nothing but permafrost and tree-covered hills as far as the eye could see. The desolate wasteland expanded a thousand kilometers east of Lake Baikal. During the previous three hours, Sokolov had encountered no signs of civilization. Only the lifeless remains of a few decaying villages stood in the vicinity of the railroad.

"Approaching target coordinates," Zubov announced. "I've got visual contact."

When Sokolov spotted the train with his own eyes, there was no more room for doubt.

The drab-green-colored 2M62 power unit was hauling a string of fifty-six freight cars, but only twenty-seven of those were standard boxcars. The rest of the train consisted of cylindrical tank cars, each filled with fifty cubic meters of liquefied natural gas.

With the pipeline to North Korea still years away from completion, Russian gas exports relied on transporting LNG tanks by rail.

Number 4001 was traveling with an escort. A private train followed it close behind. Another M62 locomotive pulling five passenger carriages. The middle car had an image painted on its side. An icon of the Mother of God. It was a chapel car, Sokolov realized, one of the many used by the Moscow Patriarchate.

Sokolov joined Zubov and Mischenko in the cockpit.

"What on earth is this?" Mischenko asked in the pilot's seat. "Some sort of a mobile church?"

"Yeah, but that's a false front. I bet it's heavily armored and jam-packed with communications equipment. These trains are traveling in the typical formation favored by North Korean defense forces. Their Train Escort Division usually operates a group of three trains. The main train is followed by the train carrying the security staff. There should also be a scout train—a single locomotive running ten minutes ahead to check the safety of the rail tracks."

"So, one of the cars has a nuclear bomb on board?" Zubov asked.

"Let's find out. Yuri, bring us within range."

Mischenko tilted the stick, easing the chopper to an altitude of two hundred meters.

Sokolov spoke into the mic of the 450-Watt, six-horn loudhailer system.

"Attention! This is EMERCOM of Russia. You are requested to stop immediately for inspection. I repeat, stop immediately. Failure to comply will result in the use of deadly force."

The freight train didn't look like slowing down. As the helicopter circled toward the church train to deliver Sokolov's final warning, a hail of machine-gun fire erupted from the windows of the passenger cars.

Bullets punctured the fuselage, punching holes in the chopper's outer skin.

Mischenko yanked the controls. The Ka-32 banked sharply, gaining altitude.

"That was close!" Mischenko said.

"Deadly force? So much for your bluff, Gene. Perhaps you should have talked to them in Korean instead," Zubov quipped.

"It was worth a try. We've got them dead to rights now."

"What's your plan? Don't tell me you're going to hijack the freight train!"

"No, I'm not that crazy. I wouldn't think about hijacking a train guarded by an army of goons and loaded with enough LNG to blow up a city," Sokolov said. "I'm going to derail it."

Zubov and Mischenko exchanged quizzical glances.

"But it has to be done *now*, while we're in the middle of the tundra," Sokolov explained. "The window of opportunity is too small. Stopping these bastards will come at the cost of radioactive pollution, so we can't allow them to reach populated areas like Khabarovsk or Vladivostok."

"Whatever you say."

His team-mates trusted him with their lives unconditionally.

The Ka-32 hit its cruising speed of 230 km/h. Three minutes later, it gained on the scout train, which was running in advance just like Sokolov had predicted.

"What's the lowest altitude you can hover at?" Sokolov asked Mischenko.

"Twenty-five meters."

"Gonna try your luck with another public announcement?" Zubov mused.

"Almost. Neither of you guessed the correct answer but Yuri came closer. It's the scout train that I'm going to hijack."

"Are you kidding?"

"I wish I were. Weather conditions?"

"Minus twenty-five degrees Celsius. Wind gusts up to nine meters per second, north-north-west," Zubov replied.

"Could be worse," Sokolov said as he went aft.

He zipped up his parka, adjusted the fur-lined hood, and put on a pair of leather gloves and ski goggles. Then he grabbed a standard-issue AK rifle and slung over his shoulder. He recalled the story Constantine had told him. Like the nuclear bomb, the famed Kalashnikov rifle had been stolen by the Soviets from Germany. At the end of the Second World War, the Red Army had seized the legendary weapons developer Hugo Schmeisser with ten thousand pages of his research. Alongside fifteen other captive German engineers, he'd been forced to complete his work on a new submachine gun, now known as the AK-47. As the prototype neared production, communist propaganda would have suffered a terrible blow if the involvement of Schmeisser's group of German specialists had ever become known. Thus the lie had originated. The design of the rifle had been attributed to some illiterate peasant named Mikhail Kalashnikov, who'd shamelessly claimed it as his own. The man had been a fraud his entire life. In effect, the AK owed its reliability to German quality triumphing over Soviet manufacture. And reliability in the harshest environments was exactly what Sokolov wanted.

Sokolov lacked the Navy SEAL training to rappel from the chopper, Hollywood style, but thankfully he wouldn't need to pull off such a stunt. Instead, he had the luxury of a rescue basket which came as part of the Kamov's firefighting equipment. The rescue basket had a rigid frame capable of holding two passengers. Resembling a window-cleaning cradle, it was utilized for the rooftop evacuation of victims from burning high-rise buildings.

He slid open the port side door. An icy gust blew a flurry of snowflakes inside. Twenty-five meters below, the scout train charged along the tracks. Mischenko was keeping the chopper level with the driver's cabin of the locomotive.

Sokolov latched the rescue basket's lifting harness on to the hook of the electric winch and pushed it clear. The cable hoist suspended it from the side of the helicopter.

Sokolov stepped onto the platform of the rescue basket, climbed in and sat down, holding on to the rigid frame. He pressed a switch and the electric motor whirred, lowering the basket. It descended at a rate of two meters per second, swaying and bobbing, edging closer to the locomotive. The wind howled, picking up flurries of snow whipped up by the helicopter's thumping rotors. Flying parallel to the scout train, Mischenko maneuvered the chopper with surgical precision.

Sokolov gripped the AK, thumbed the safety lever down, and pulled the charging handle, chambering a round.

From the sitting position inside the dangling basket, he struggled to maintain balance as he brought the stock to his shoulder. He steadied his breathing to the rhythm of the locomotive's rattling wheels. Mischenko had brought the basket within a couple of meters of the scout train. From such a close distance, the driver's cabin was impossible to miss. The cabin was so near that Sokolov managed to see his adversary through the side window.

A North Korean soldier in winter uniform was sitting at the controls. His peripheral vision caught the tethered basket looming outside. His head jerked in surprise a moment before he met his death.

Sokolov squeezed the trigger. The AK chattered on full auto, spitting fire from its muzzle. The 5.45x39mm rounds tore through the driver's cabin, piercing steel and smashing glass as Sokolov emptied the magazine. He ejected it and snapped a fresh one into the receiver with an audible click.

Slinging the AK diagonally across his back, he drew himself up. Precariously, he leaned forward, placing a foot over the top tube of the frame. Pushing his body away from the basket, he propelled himself toward the train.

In mid-air, his heart froze for a split second as he felt that his leap was destined to fail and he would crash against the ground. With the agility of an Olympic gymnast, he clutched the handrails outside the driver's door with his fingertips. Swinging his legs, he got a foothold on the loop step below. Hanging on one-handed, he pulled open the bullet-riddled door and jumped inside.

The heated train cabin reeked of gore and motor oil. The dead driver sat sagging behind the steering wheel, red patches of blood surrounding the bullet holes in his head and chest. The Trans-Siberian Railway wasn't safe for North Koreans, after all.

The scout train was still chugging along the tracks. Sokolov gave the ancient instrument panel a quick glance. He only had a vague idea of the meaning of each gauge and dial, but his general knowledge of train operation would have to suffice. The speedometer needle jittered at the 30 km/h mark. Sokolov threw the master controller handle from acceleration to braking. The train decelerated, wheels squealing, but the drop in velocity wasn't sharp enough. Sokolov pushed the emergency brake button. The locomotive shuddered as it came to a complete halt. Staying on his feet, he twisted the bezel of his Breitling to mark the time.

Sokolov had only gotten the job half-done. Next, he shifted the gear into reverse and set the controller handle to acceleration. As the 2000-horsepower diesel pushed the 120-ton locomotive into backward motion, Sokolov rushed to the door and hopped out of the cabin. He somersaulted to cushion his landing on the rock-hard frozen earth, and sprang to his feet.

The Kamov buzzed, floating in the air a few meters away, ready to scoop him up with the rescue basket. Sokolov sprinted toward it. Every second counted. Reaching it, he hauled himself over the frame and collapsed onto the solid platform in a heap. No sooner had he scrambled into it than the rescue basket lifted off the ground, tugged by the rapidly-ascending Kamov.

He hadn't dragged himself over the finish line just yet. The Ka-32 had to gain maximum distance, breaking away from the railroad. Sokolov's breathing came in ragged puffs of vapor. The basket pitched and swayed as the electric winch hoisted it at full speed. Once it drew level with the helicopter door, Zubov snatched Sokolov by the lapel of his parka and yanked him inside the chopper. They both toppled onto the deck.

"Watch it! You're choking me!"

Zubov groaned. "I'm glad that you're fitter than Mischenko, but I'm not doing this ever again. Find someone else to literally drag your hide out of the fire next time."

"If there is a next time. The fire won't get us but we might still die from the radiation."

"Love your optimism," said Zubov, getting up.

He hurried back to the co-pilot's seat.

The engines roared.

Sokolov flicked his wrist, checking the chronometer as he made a rough calculation. The ten-minute delay between the scout train and the LNG freighter meant that the time would be cut in half if they traveled on a collision course. He'd managed to get back into the chopper inside ninety seconds, so he estimated that the crash would occur in three more minutes. The chopper should be ten kilometers away by that time.

Despite his fatigue, Sokolov rose, pulled the rescue basket back in and slammed the door shut. At the port window, he watched the tundra recede from view as the Ka-32 climbed to cruising altitude.

He counted down the seconds, thanking the Lord for their escape to safety as a flash streaked across the horizon.

18

The train crash left no survivors.

The freight train was coming out of a curve when the two-man crew suddenly saw the scout train closing in at full speed. They engaged the hand brakes, trying to restrain the freighter's momentum, but nothing could have prevented the collision. The two trains rammed into each other head-on. The impact heaved the scout locomotive skyward and killed the crew inside the freight train's cabin, turning it into a mass of corrugated metal. The diesel caught fire immediately.

In a chain reaction, forty of the fifty-six freight cars derailed, including the tank cars which rolled sideways. Almost every tank car was breached, spilling liquefied gas.

A mist of vaporizing gas shrouded the wreckage.

The freight locomotive had broken free from the rest of the train. The fire from the burning diesel ignited the leak, blowing up fifteen hundred cubic meters of LNG.

A series of explosions quaked the Siberian tundra. Gigantic fireballs erupted in quick succession, the flames shooting more than fifty meters high. The approaching church train was engulfed in flames before any of its occupants knew what hit them.

The LNG detonation created a blast radius of over one kilometer.

The radioactive contamination from the destroyed nuclear device was spreading even farther.

19

The Patriarch of Lubyanka banged his fist against the mahogany table.

"What is the meaning of this?"

Spittle flew from Galaktion's mouth.

"I'm asking you, Saveliy Ignatievich! Care to explain?"

The mood inside the Red Room was less than jovial compared to their previous meeting.

"Nobody knows for certain how it happened," Frolov replied. "It's too early to reconstruct the chronology of the accident. Only a full investigation will reveal all the details. At the moment, preliminary findings show that the trains somehow crashed into one another. The resulting fire caused a massive explosion. It prompted a response from emergency crews, who arrived on the scene within a few hours. The Defense Minister has privately told me that they detected traces of radioactive pollution. A red zone has been cordoned off and huge numbers of EMERCOM and Army personnel have moved in to secure the area. All trains running on the Trans-Siberian Railway have been cancelled indefinitely."

"Do they have anything that may put the blame on me? Any incriminating evidence?"

"Nothing so far. They've recovered several bodies from the wreckage."

"What bodies? Can any of them be identified and linked to the Patriarchate?"

"No, Your Holiness. The train convoy was one hundred percent North Korean."

"To hell with the North Koreans! Incompetent bastards, the lot of them. Where's the damned bomb? Did it remain intact?"

"It was aboard the freight train when the liquefied gas detonated."

Galaktion's bloodshot eyes watered.

"Operation Temple is finished," he uttered ruefully.

"It's gone up in smoke, so to speak. We must regroup."

The Patriarch pointed a crooked, arthritic finger at Frolov.

"You ... you ...! It's all *your* fault! You dragged me into this! You told me that the plan was foolproof! And now you want to back out?"

"Don't forget yourself, you old fool. Nobody could have predicted such a force-majeure event as a train derailment. It was an act of God."

"Your irony is inappropriate," Galaktion said through gritted teeth. "Did your man retrieve the Oltersdorf books, at least?"

"No. He's vanished without trace. And so have the papers, as well as the girl."

"It's unacceptable! I made promises to some very dangerous people. This setback makes me more vulnerable than ever."

"There are few people more dangerous than me. I also gave my word to men in high places. We may have lost the battle, but not the war. I prepared for any eventuality, no matter how outlandish. Trust me, I've got all bases covered."

Cooling off, the Patriarch asked, "So, what's your backup plan?"

"Damage control is the first priority. Thankfully, keeping the whole affair under wraps won't be a problem. The Kremlin has already enforced a media lockdown on the rail disaster story. My FSB ties will help me influence the investigation to make sure that your name never crops up."

"And after that?"

"We're still in this together. Despite our failure to transform Russia into a theocracy, I count on your continued support. We have every chance of seizing power by other means. It'll take more time and effort, but with your commitment nothing is impossible."

"I'm listening."

"I'll need your money, human resources, and above all, your public backing."

"We've known each other for a long time. Throughout the years, you've always avoided publicity. What scheme would require it, all of a sudden? Saveliy, don't tell me that you're plotting a revolution."

"Why, we live in a free and democratic society. The Constitution says that any Russian over the age of thirty-five can be elected as the country's President. Your Holiness, may I have your blessing to run for office?"

EPILOGUE

We are fighting against the Bolsheviks in a mortal struggle which cannot end in a treaty or an agreement, for in this fight we are protecting the Motherland against The International, freedom against tyranny, and culture against savagery.

—Admiral Alexander Kolchak, July 1919

The three-man council convened in the sanctuary of the government office opposite the Bolshoi. The secret meeting continued long into the night as its participants decided the fate of the gold treasure.

Each of the three group members had just returned to Moscow: Constantine, who'd recovered from injuries; Eugene, whose blood tests had shown no radiation exposure; and Nikolai Klimov, back after his inspection of the disaster area on the Trans-Siberian Railway.

As the senior man, it was the general who had the final say on the matter.

Constantine read out the Oltersdorf statement in full. He'd spent the previous week holed up in the mobile command unit, decoding the notebook by hand. It was an extraordinary document. Of all the theories surrounding the mystery of the lost gold, the evidence revealed by Peter Oltersdorf confirmed the wildest one.

With the city of Omsk, the capital of Kolchak's government, about to fall to the Bolsheviks, the Admiral had ordered the evacuation of the gold reserve. Gold bullion worth 250,000,000 rubles had been loaded into wagons and sent across the frozen Lake Baikal. The winter of 1920 had been particularly harsh, with temperatures dropping below -60 degrees Celsius. The caravan had frozen to death crossing the world's largest lake. The coming of spring had thawed the ice, sending the gold-laden caravan to its watery grave.

The remainder of Kolchak's treasury had been transferred to pay for the support of the Allies: monies allotted for military procurement but never spent. The funds had been accruing interest across numerous accounts in British, French, American, and Japanese banks. Baron Oltersdorf had provided a detailed list of every bank and every account.

"A century later, there's little chance of winning any legal battle against these financial institutions," Constantine concluded. "After the revolution, the Soviet government declared all of the financial obligations of the Russian Empire null and void. Technically, the Russian Federation is the successor of the USSR. As a rightful heiress, Stacie could file a lawsuit and try to claim the accounts held by Peter Oltersdorf personally, but I think her case would be difficult."

"She's home safe, and that's the only thing that matters to me," Eugene said. "I'm glad she's no longer burdened by these notebooks, which fell upon her like a curse."

"Or perhaps a blessing in disguise. Without the Oltersdorf legacy, you would never have met."

"True. God works in mysterious ways."

"The gold caravan," said Klimov. "Did it really sink to the bottom of Lake Baikal?"

Constantine put aside the sheaf of papers.

"The hunt for the Russian gold started way back under Stalin. And by the 1970s, the KGB had already searched Lake Baikal for the gold. They wouldn't have mounted an expedition without sufficient proof that the gold was located there. But without the exact coordinates, they failed to discover it. The bullion is more than a legend. It's real and tangible, and now we know where to look for it."

Silence fell. Klimov was lost in thought and the Sokolov brothers awaited his verdict.

"It's within my capacity as the EMERCOM Minister to set up a salvage operation. The *Mir* submersibles can reach the deepest point of Lake Baikal. If the gold is really there, we will find it. And yet ... I believe that the Oltersdorf secret should not leave these four walls."

Eugene nodded in agreement. "Even if we did salvage it, the gold would ultimately fall into the hands of Frolov, Galaktion and their ilk."

The decision was unanimous.

"The gold belongs to Russia," said Constantine. "Not the Russian government or the Russian people, but the Russian Empire which died fighting communism. We shall let it rest in her crypt."

Made in the USA
Lexington, KY
06 December 2018